ホガース「カレーの門」(1749)
本文P.203

もう一つの18世紀英詩選

和田敏英著

開文社出版

香住ヶ丘と竜王山へ

目　　次

序 …………………………………………… i

I　隠栖の詩
1　'beatus ille' 詩の背景 ………………………… 1
2　John Pomfret, 'The Choice' ……………………… 2

II　ロンドン詩
1　John Gay, 'Trivia' ……………………………19
2　Mary Robinson, 'London's Summer Morning' …24
3　Anonymous, 'A Description of the Spring in London' ……………………………………28

III　風刺の詩
1　Anon., 'The Vicar of Bray' …………………………32
2　John Collier, 'The Pluralist and Old Soldier' ……39
3　Soame Jenyns, 'The Modern Fine Gentleman' …42
　　'The Modern Fine Lady' ………………………44

IV　賛美歌
1　Isaac Watts, 'The Day of Judgement' ……………47
　　'Crucifixion to the World by the Cross of Christ' ……………………………………52

2　Charles Wesley, 'Resurrection'……………………54
　　　　'Come on, my Partners in Distress'…………………56
Ⅴ　ロマン詩
　　　1　Anne Finch, Countess of Winchilsea, 'A
　　　　Nocturnal Reverie' ……………………………63
　　　2　George, Lord Lyttelton, 'To the Memory of a
　　　　Lady: A Monody' ………………………………68
Ⅵ　物語詩
　　　1　Frances Seymour, Countess of Hertford, 'The
　　　　Story of Inkle and Yarico' ……………………81
　　　2　Lady Anne Lindsay (*later* Barnard), 'Auld
　　　　Robin Gray' ……………………………………90
Ⅶ　動物愛の詩
　　　1　Robert Burns, 'To a Mouse' ………………………96
　　　2　John Dyer, 'My Ox Duke' ………………………101
Ⅷ　フェミニズムの詩
　　　1　Mary, Lady Chudleigh, 'To the Ladies' …………106
　　　2　Mary Leapor, 'Upon her Play being returned
　　　　to her, stained with Claret'……………………109
　　　　'An Essay on Woman' …………………………112
Ⅸ　続フェミニズムの詩
　　　1　Ann Murry, 'The Tête à Tête, or Fashionable
　　　　Pair. An Eclogue' ………………………………117
　　　2　Jane West, 'To a Friend on her Marriage' ………131
Ⅹ　社会派の詩
　　　1　Hannah More, 'Slavery, A Poem' …………………138

    2 Helen Maria Williams, 'To Dr. Moore, in Answer to a Poetical Epistle Written by Him in Wales' ……………142
    3 Joseph Cottle, 'Malvern Hills' ……………152
XI 労働の詩
    1 Stephen Duck, 'The Thresher's Labour' …………157
    2 Mary Collier, 'The Woman's Labour' ……………164
    3 Christopher Smart, 'A Morning-Piece, or, An Hymn for the Hay-Makers' ……………170
XII 貧窮の詩
    1 Mary Barber, 'On seeing an Officer's Widow distracted,…' ……………177
    2 Thomas Moss, 'The Beggar' ……………181
    3 Anonymous, 'Between an Unemployed Artist and his Wife' ……………186
XIII 愛国歌
    1 Henry Fielding, 'The Roast Beef of Old England' ……………201
    2 James Thomson, 'Rule Britannia' ……………203
    3 Tobias Smollett, 'The Tears of Scotland. Written in the Year 1746' ……………208

あとがき ……………219

索　引 ……………221

序

　もはや半世紀も前のことになるが，伝統的な 18 世紀英詩観を作りあげた研究書の一つは James Sutherland の名講義録『18 世紀詩序文』（*A Preface to Eighteenth Century Poetry, 1948*）ではなかろうか．すなわち，サザランド教授は，王政復古の 1660 年をもって新しい知的風土の出発点とし，その文化状況全般を Hobbes, Newton, Locke たち 3 巨人の視座のもとに，理性，普遍，保守，安定，秩序，品位，美への時代志向を指摘し，おもに上流社会の教養人士のために良き文学として Mock-heroic や詩語を多用しつつも，抑制（Restraint）と洗練（Refinement）を 18 世紀英詩の二大特徴として講じたのであった．

　したがって，この時代には奇矯，反社会的，曖昧，不確かで不規則な詩風が排斥され，Dryden に始まる Pope や Johnson たちの風刺詩，それに Gray や Thomson たち，つまり文学史のいわゆる Pre-Romantics の自然詩が 18 世紀英詩の正典として考えられてきたといえるであろう．

　しかし，いま 18 世紀英詩にもようやく新しい見直しの時機が到来した．これまで詩壇の主流から取り残され，社会の片隅で日の目を見なかった不遇の詩作者たちの作品が脚光を浴びる

ようになったのである．たとえば，David Nichol Smith 編の旧版『オックスフォード 18 世紀詩集』（*The Oxford Book of Eighteenth Century Verse*, 1926）をほぼ 60 年ぶり大幅に改訂した Roger Lonsdale 編の『新オックスフォード 18 世紀詩集』（*The New Oxford Book of Eighteenth Century Verse*, 1984）や『18 世紀女流詩人たち，オックスフォード詞華集』（*Eighteenth-Century Women Poets: An Oxford Anthology*, 1989），また Robert W. Uphaus と Gretchen M. Foster 共編の『「別」の 18 世紀，イギリス女性作家たち 1660－1800』（*The "Other" Eighteenth Century. English Women of Letters 1660-1800*, East Lansing: Colleagues Press, 1991）など，その動向の証拠となるであろう．以下，英詩にかぎらず，新しい視点で編まれた詩文選のささやかなリストを揚げておこう．

1 *Before Their Time: Six Women Writers of the Eighteenth Century*, edited by Katharine M. Rogers (New York; Frederick Ungar Publishing Co., 1979).

2 *Feminism in Eighteenth-Century England*, edited by Katharine M. Rogers (University of Illinois Press, 1982).

3 *Eighteenth-Century Women: An Anthology*, edited by Bridget Hill (London; George Allen & Unwin, 1984).

4 *Poetry By English Women: Elizabethan to Victorian*, edited by R.E. Pritchard (The Continuum Publishing Company, 1990).

5 *Women in the Eighteenth Century: Constructions of femininity*, edited by Vivien Jones (London and New York;

Routledge, 1990).

6 *Women, Writing, History 1640-1740,* edited by Isobel Grundy & Susan Wiseman (The University of Georgia Press, 1992).

7 *Romantic Women Poets 1770-1838: An Anthology,* edited by Andrew Ashfield (Manchester University Press, 1995).

8 *Eighteenth-Century Poetry. An Annotated Anthology,* edited by David Fairer and Christine Gerrard (Blackwell Publishers, 1998).

　当然のことながら，詩人層の拡大は目ざましく，とくに散文を含めた女性作家たちの活躍は注目に値しよう．青鞜派グループはもちろんのこと，牛乳売りの女，洗濯女，農民すら詩作していたのである．さまざまな社会階層出身の詩作者たちが取りあげる題材は，田舎や都会，恋愛や結婚，宗教や政治などのテーマに加えて，ゴルフ，催眠術，動物，労働，失業，貧困，政変，フランス革命，奴隷制度と多岐にわたり，かれらは因襲にとらわれず，生き生きと，ユーモラスに詩を書いたのである．

　このように眺めてみると，18世紀の英詩は，Milton (1606-74) と Wordsworth (1770-1850) と，二つの巨峰に挟まれた谷間にあるとする従来の観点からだけでは，その豊かさを捉えきれないであろう．伝統的な正典のほかに，もう一つの18世紀英詩の姿が検討されてもよいのではなかろうか．

I 隠栖の詩

1 'beatus ille' 詩の背景

12歳頃の少年 Pope (1688-1744) が「孤独の頌 ('Ode on Solitude', *c*.1700) と称する隠栖礼賛の詩を書いたのは, 早熟な老成のためというよりは, 古典詩 Horatius の 'Epode II' の模倣によるところが大きかった. 例の「幸せなるかな, かかる人は…」('Beatus ille qui...', Happy the man who...) のような常套句をもつ詩は 17 世紀から 18 世紀前半にかけて頻出しており, ノルウェーの Maren-Sofie Røstvig の大著 *The Happy man: Studies in the Metamorphoses of a Classical Ideal, 1600-1760* (Oxford, 1954-58, 2 vols., Vol. I, rev. 1962) によって詳しく実証されている.

実際, ポープの前にも, とりわけ Abraham Cowley (1618-67) の「願望」('The Wish', 1647) や自伝的エッセー「私自身について」('Of My Self', 1668) などは, 隠栖のテーマを顕著に謳っている.[1]

確かに, 都市の喧騒や権謀術数の渦巻く宮廷を離れて, よき友と書に囲まれ, 美しい自然のなかで, 悠々と静かな生涯を終えるのが古典的な理想の生き方であったが, しかし何故この時期に田園生活の理想化や隠栖が謳歌されたのであろうか.

国威の発揚したエリザベス朝時代ならば，超人的な性格の持ち主が理想的人間像としてふさわしかったであろう．たとえば，Christopher Marlowe (1564-93) の一連の劇作品，*Tamburlaine the Great, Doctor Faustus, The Jew of Malta* をみても，それぞれ征服欲，知識欲，物欲の権化のような主人公は，まさしくルネッサンスの時代精神を反映したものにちがいない．

ところが17世紀となると，清教徒革命，王政復古，名誉革命と社会の激動が続き，時代の混迷と不安は深く，野望に燃えた強烈な個性を持つ巨人は，もはや理想的人物ではなく，むしろ危険きわまる存在となったであろう．「狂熱」('enthusiasm') という言葉が象徴するように，次なる18世紀社会の趨勢は，その抑制と沈静，平和と安定へと推移したといえるのではなかろうか．「隠退の神話」が生まれる理由の一つはこの辺りにあると思われる．

2　John Pomfret, 'The Choice'

さて，隠栖の詩の典型的な作品といえば，やはり新旧の『オックスフォード18世紀詩集』の冒頭を飾るジョン・ポムフリット (1667-1702) の「選択」('The Choice', 1700)[2] を挙げなくてはなるまい．全篇167行，煩をいとわず，原詩に詩訳を添えてみよう．

The Choice

If Heav'n the Grateful Liberty wou'd give,
That I might Chuse my Method how to Live,

I 隠栖の詩

And all those Hours, propitious Fate should lend,
In blissful Ease, and Satisfaction spend:
  Near some fair Town, I'd have a private Seat,
Built Uniform, not Little, nor too Great:
Better, if on a Rising Ground it stood;
Fields on this side, on that a Neighbouring Wood.
It shou'd within no other Things contain,
But what were Useful, Necessary, Plain: 10
Methinks 'tis Nauseous, and I'd ne'er endure
The needless Pomp of Gaudy Furniture.
A little Garden, Grateful to the Eye,
And a Cool Rivulet run murm'ring by:
On whose delicious Banks a stately Row
Of Shady Limes, or Sycamores, shou'd grow:
At th' End of which a silent Study plac'd,
Shou'd be with all the Noblest Authors Grac'd:
Horace, and *Virgil,* in whose Mighty Lines
Immortal Wit, and Solid Learning shines; 20
Sharp *Juvenal,* and Am'rous *Ovid* too,
Who all the Turns of Love's soft Passion knew;
He that with Judgment reads his charming Lines,
In which strong Art, with stronger Nature joyns,
Must grant his Fancy does the best Excel,
His Thoughts so tender, and Exprest so well;
With all those Moderns, Men of steady Sense,
Esteem'd for Learning, and for Eloquence.

In some of these, as Fancy shou'd Advise,
30　　I'd always take my Morning Exercise:
For sure no Minutes bring us more Content,
Than those in Pleasing, Useful Studies spent.

もし神が快い自由を下さるならば，
生きる仕方を選べとて，
そうして優しい運命が貸して下さるその時を
至福に満ちて過ごせ，とて．
　どこか美しい町にほど近く，ひっそりとした屋敷を構えよう．
造りはむらなく，小さくはなく，また大き過ぎもせず，
高台に建つならさらによい．
かたや野が，かたや林が隣り合う．
屋内に入れるべき物とては
10　有用必須で地味なもの．
思うに，厭で耐えられぬ
豪華な家具の無用な飾り．
小さな庭は，目に快く，
涼しい小川が囁き流れ，
楽しい土手には堂々とした並木
陰なす菩提樹，カエデが育つ．
端には静かな書斎を設け，
一流作家で飾らせる．
ホラスにヴァージル，力漲る詩の行に
20　不滅の機知と学が輝く．

I　隠栖の詩

鋭いジュヴェナル，それに多情のオヴィッドも，
恋の綾ならみな心得て.
魅惑の詩行を熟読すれば,
技巧にまさる天来の妙,
空想の飛翔は群を抜く,
想いはやさしく，巧みな表現.
堅実な思慮ある現代作家も友とする,
学と弁，衆に秀でた人たちならば.
気の向くままに，この幾人と
朝稽古，いつも怠らぬことにする.　　　　　　　　　　30
というわけは，これほどに心の満ちる時はない,
楽しくて益ある研究の時なれば.　　　　　　(ll.1-32)

　I'd have a Clear, and Competent Estate,
That I might Live Gentilely, but not Great:
As much as I cou'd moderately spend,
A little more, sometimes t' Oblige a Friend.
Nor shou'd the Sons of Poverty Repine
Too much at Fortune, they shou'd Taste of mine;
And all, that Objects of true Pitty were,
Shou'd be Reliev'd with what my Wants cou'd spare　40
For what, our Maker has too largely giv'n,
Shou'd be return'd, in Gratitude, to Heav'n.
A frugal Plenty shou'd my Table spread;
With Healthy, not Luxurious Dishes Fed:
Enough to Satisfy, and something more

To Feed the Stranger, and the Neighb'ring Poor.
Strong Meat Indulges Vice, and pampering Food
Creates Diseases, and Inflames the Blood.
But what's sufficient to make Nature strong,
50　And the bright Lamp of Life continue long,
I'd freely take, and as I did Possess,
The Bounteous Author of my Plenty Bless.

　抵当に入っておらず，よい収入を生む地所を手に入れよう．
優雅な暮らしができるよう，豪奢な暮らしはさておいて．
費やす金はつつましく，
友を迎えては惜しみなく．
貧民に悲運の嘆きは言わせまい，
恵まれたこちらの運を味あわせ．
まことに哀れな者たちは
40　節約分で助けよう．
造物主から気前よく貰ったものは
感謝して神に戻すが人の道．
食卓はつましいうちにもたっぷりと，
健康によく，贅沢でない料理をあてがおう．
満ち足ればよく，それ以上のものは
見知らぬ人と近隣の貧しい人に与えよう．
味濃い食事は悪癖をつのらせ，飽食は
病気をつくり，血をほてらせる．
だがしかし，身体を丈夫にするものや，

生命の輝く灯火を絶やさぬものは，
存分に摂取して，これまで享受したように，
わが豊かさの恵み深い造り主を祝福しよう．(ll.33-52)

  I'd have a little Vault, but always stor'd
With the Best Wines, each Vintage cou'd afford.
Wine whets the Wit, improves its Native force,
And gives a pleasant Flavour to Discourse;
By making all our Spirits Debonair,
Throws off the Lees, the Sediment of Care.
But as the greatest Blessing, Heaven lends,
May be Debauch'd, and serve Ignoble Ends:
So, but too oft, the Grape's refreshing Juice
Does many Mischievous Effects produce.
My House shou'd no such rude Disorders know,
As from high Drinking consequently flow.
Nor wou'd I use, what was so kindly giv'n,
To the Dishonour of Indulgent Heav'n.
If any Neighbour came, he shou'd be Free,
Us'd with Respect, and not uneasy be,
In my Retreat, or to himself, or me.
What Freedom, Prudence, and right Reason give,
All Men may with Impunity receive:
But the least swerving from their Rule's too much:
For, what's forbidden us, 'tis Death to touch.

8

　　　わたしは小さな地下蔵を持とう，だが貯えはいつも
　　作柄ごと最良の葡萄酒にして．
　　葡萄酒は才覚を研ぎ澄まし，その本来の力を強め，
　　会話に楽しい風味を添える．
　　気持ちをすっかり晴れやかにして，
　　酒粕の苦労の澱(おり)は投げ捨てる．
　　だがしかし，神の最たる祝福とても
60　汚されて恥ずべき役をしたりする．
　　そのように，だが頻繁に，清涼な葡萄酒も
　　多くの災禍を作り出す．
　　わが家にかかる無頼は許すまい，
　　飲めや歌えに付き物の．
　　そしてまた天与のものを無駄にしては
　　優しい神の名に傷がつく．
　　もし隣人の客あれば，のびのびと寛ろがせ，
　　敬意をもって待遇し，窮屈な思いは露させぬ，
　　わが隠宅で，客人ともに己れにも．
70　自由と思慮と理性とが与えるものは
　　人みなが難なく無事に受け取れる．
　　だがしかし，この掟から少しでも逸れてしまえば一大事，
　　禁に触れるは死罪ゆえ．　　　　　　　(ll.53-73)

　　That Life might be more Comfortable yet,
　　And all my Joys Refin'd, Sincere, and Great;
　　I'd Chuse two Friends, whose Company wou'd be
　　A great Advance to my Felicity:

Well Born, of Humours suited to my own,
Discreet, and Men, as well as Books, have known:
Brave, Gen'rous, Witty, and exactly Free   80
From loose Behaviour, or Formality;
Airy, and Prudent, Merry, but not Light,
Quick in Discerning, and in Judging right.
Secret they shou'd be, Faithful to their Trust;
In Reas'ning Cool, Strong, Temperate, and Just;
Obliging, Open, without Huffing Brave,
Brisk in Gay Talking, and in Sober, Grave;
Close in Dispute, but not Tenacious, try'd
By Solid Reason, and let that Decide;
Not prone to Lust, Revenge, or Envious Hate,   90
Nor busy Medlers with Intreagues of State;
Strangers to Slander, and sworn Foes to Spight,
Not Quarrelsome, but Stout enough to Fight;
Loyal, and Pious, Friends to *Cæsar* true,
As Dying Martyrs to their Maker too;
In their Society, I cou'd not miss
A Permanent, Sincere, Substantial Bliss.

　人生がもっと快適となるように,
喜びが洗練されて, 表裏なく, 大きなものとなるように,
2人の友を選びたい, その付き合いで
わが幸せが増すだろう.
生まれよく, こちらの気質にもぴったりで,

慎み深く，書物と人間が分かる人．
80 勇敢で，寛大で，機知に富み，その上に
不品行，堅苦しさが微塵もなくて，
軽快だが慎重で，陽気だが軽率でなく，
眼識は鋭く，判断に間違いがない．
口は堅くて，信頼に応えられ，
推論は冷静，確固，中庸を得て公正，
丁重で隠し立てなく，威張ることなく勇敢で，
陽気な話には活発で，真面目な話では厳粛で，
議論は厳密，だが固執せず，立証は
堅実な理性によって，それで決着，
90 好色，復讐，また嫉妬深い憎悪に傾かず，
はたまたお節介な大陰謀にも立ち入らぬ．
中傷を知らず，遺恨とは不倶戴天の敵，
喧嘩は嫌うが，戦えば手強い．
忠誠にして敬虔，まことの君主の味方．誠実は
死に臨む殉教者のごとく，造物主に対しても同じ．
かかる人との交際で，見逃すことはあり得まい，
永久の，まことの，実のある幸福を． (ll.74-97)

    Wou'd Bounteous Heav'n once more Indulge, I'd choose,
(For who wou'd so much Satisfaction lose,
100 As Witty Nymphs, in Conversation, give,)
Near some Obliging, Modest Fair to live;
For there's that Sweetness in a Female Mind,

Which in a Man's we cannot hope to find:
That by a Secret, but a Pow'rful, Art
Winds up the Springs of Life, and does impart
Fresh Vital Heat to the Transported Heart.

  I'd have her Reason all her Passions sway;
Easy in Company, in Private Gay:
Coy to a Fop, to the Deserving Free,
Still Constant to her self, and Just to me. 110
A Soul she shou'd have, for Great Actions fit;
Prudence, and Wisdom to direct her Wit:
Courage to look bold Danger in the Face,
No Fear, but only to be Proud, or Base:
Quick to Advise, by an Emergence prest,
To give good Counsel, or to take the best.
I'd have th' Expression of her Thoughts be such,
She might not seem Reserv'd, nor talk too much;
That shews a want of Judgment and of Sense:
More than Enough is but Impertinence: 120
Her Conduct Regular, her Mirth Refin'd,
Civil to Strangers, to her Neighbours kind:
Averse to Vanity, Revenge, and Pride,
In all the Methods of Deceit untry'd:
So Faithful to her Friend, and Good to all,
No Censure might upon her Actions fall:
Then wou'd e'en Envy be compell'd to say,
She goes the least of Woman-kind Astray.

To this Fair Creature I'd sometimes Retire;
130 Her Conversation wou'd new Joys inspire;
Give Life an Edge so keen, no surly Care
Would venture to Assault my Soul, or dare
Near my Retreat to hide one secret Snare.
But so Divine, so Noble a Repast,
I'd seldom, and with Moderation, taste.
For Highest Cordials all their Virtue lose,
By a too frequent, and too bold an Use:
And what wou'd Cheer the Spirits in Distress,
Ruines our Health, when taken to Excess.

　寛大な神がもう一度，気ままにさせて下さるならば，
　（機知ある乙女らが，話上手に与えてくれる
100 それほど多くの満足を失いたい者はいない筈だから，）
世話好きで，淑やかな美女のもとにて暮らしたい．
女の心にはあの優しさがあるわけで，
男の心にはとても見つからぬ優しさだ．
その優しさが，ひっそりと，だが強い力で
命のバネを引き締めて，与えてくれる
恍惚境に新たな気力．
　彼女の情熱はその理性に支配させ，
付き合いにはくつろいで，私生活では快活に，
伊達男には打ち解けず，一廉(かど)の人には伸び伸びと，
110 絶えず自分に忠実で，公明正大わたしには．
持たせたい，立派な行為にかなう魂，

I　隠栖の詩

機知を導く思慮と智恵,
危難を見据える勇猛心,
恐れるものは, ただ傲慢と卑劣のみ.
危急が迫れば, 目ざとく知らせ,
良き忠告か, 最善の策.
想いを述べれば, こうでありたい,
遠慮がちにみえずとも, 喋り過ぎもせず,
さもなくば思慮分別の足らぬ証,
過ぎたるは唯の生意気. 120
振舞いは整然と, 陽気な笑いも上品に,
見知らぬ人には丁寧に, 隣人には親切に.
虚栄, 復讐, 傲慢を嫌い,
欺瞞の手管は未経験.
友に誠実, みなに親切,
彼女の行為に非難ひとつも降りかかるまい.
それだから妬みですらも認めよう.
道に迷わぬ女の鑑と.
　この美女のもとへ時々は引き籠もり,
親しく交わって喜びを新たにし, 130
生活に強い刺激を与えれば, むっつりした心労が
わが魂を襲おうとはすまい, また敢えて
わが隠れ家に近く秘密の罠を潜ませたりも.
だがしかし, これほど天来見事なご馳走は
節制をして, 滅多に味わわぬことにする.
最高の強壮剤とて効能が消えていくもの,
頻度が過ぎて無茶に使えば.

14

      滅入る気持ちを高ぶらせるものも，
      過度に耽れば身体を損なう．   (ll.98-139)

140   I'd be concern'd in no Litigious Jar,
     Belov'd by all, not vainly Popular.
     What e're Assistance I had Pow'r to bring
     T' Oblige my Country, or to Serve my King,
     When e're they Call'd, I'd readily afford
     My Tongue, my Pen, my Counsel, or my Sword.
     Law Suits I'd shun, with as much studious Care,
     As I wou'd Dens where hungry Lyons are:
     And rather put up Injuries, than be
     A Plague to him who'd be a Plague to me.
150 I value Quiet at a Price too great,
     To give for my Revenge so dear a Rate:
     For what do we, by all our Bustle, gain,
     But Counterfeit Delight, for real Pain?

140 争い事には関心を持たず，
     皆に愛され，人気を求めぬ．
     援助が要れば何にせよ，力を発揮，
     わが国のため，わが王のため，
     求められれば何時なりと，即座に揮う
     弁舌を，文筆を，忠告助言，また剣を．
     訴訟は避ける，大いに注意用心し，
     飢えたる獅子の寝ぐらと同じ．

I 隠栖の詩   15

危害を受けても我慢がましだ,
相手もろとも苦しむよりは.
平穏がこの上なく大事にて   150
復讐に高値はつけられぬ.
あたふたと騒ぎ立てても何の得,
労多くして偽の喜び.   (ll.140-53)

   If Heav'n a Date of many Years wou'd give,
Thus I'd in Pleasure, Ease, and Plenty live.
And as I near approach'd the Verge of Life,
Some kind Relation, (for I'd have no Wife)
Shou'd take upon him all my Worldly Care,
While I did for a better State prepare.
Then I'd not be with any Trouble vex'd,   160
Nor have the Ev'ning of my days perplex'd;
But by a silent, and a peaceful Death,
Without a Sigh, resign my Aged Breath:
And when committed to the Dust, I'd have
Few Tears, but Friendly, dropt into my Grave.
Then wou'd my Exit so propitious be,
All Men wou'd wish to Live, and Dye like me.
                              The Choice, 1700

   もし神が長き命を下さるならば,
このように楽しく, ゆったり, 豊かに暮らす.
そうして死期が近づけば,

誰か優しい親族に（わたしは妻を持たぬ故）
　　　この世の世話を引き受けさせる．
　　　あの世の旅に備えつつ．
160　そうなれば何の悩みにも苛立たず，
　　　わが黄昏の日にもまごつかぬ．
　　　静かで平和な死によって，
　　　溜息ひとつ吐きもせず，老いたる息をあきらめる．
　　　塵に帰れば，その時は，わたしは
　　　墓に数滴の優しい涙を垂れてもらおう．
　　　こうなればわが旅立ちは縁起よく，
　　　人皆がわが生と死を望むであろう． 　　(ll.154-67)

　このように，牧師ポムフリットは人生の自由な「選択」が許されると仮定した上で，住居，飲食，喜捨，書物，友人，女性，社交と交際，死を迎える態度など生活百般について，中庸と節度と平穏を守って生きることを理想としたのである．今日的な見方からすれば，これは消極的な生き方かもしれない．また，この詩は理想を強調するあまり，時に冗長，教訓的な説教癖もある印象を与えかねない．だが，前述したカウリーの「願望」やポープの「孤独の頌」などの道具立てが出揃った集大成となっており，以後ほぼ百年にわたり「大衆的な古典」（'a popular classic'）[3] として世に親しまれてきた理由も肯けるであろう．

　このあと隠栖テーマのアンソロジー・ピースとしては，著名な女流詩人 Anne Finch, Countess of Winchilsea の 'The Petition for an Absolute Retreat' (1713)[4] や Samuel Rogers の佳品 'A Wish' (1786)[5] などがあるが，他方で John

I 隠栖の詩   17

Philips の 'The Splendid Shilling, An Imitation of Milton' (1701)[6] や Isaac Hawkins Browne の 'The Fireside: A Pastoral Soliloquy' (1735)[7] では，'beatus ille' の常套句が早くも形骸化，パロディ化されて，換骨奪胎，隠栖の理念から次第にかけ離れていくように思われる．図式的にいえば，世紀の後半，産業革命の進展につれ，田園の荒廃現象とともに，さしもの隠栖礼賛も衰退の道を辿ることになるのではなかろうか．ただ依然として，田園風景の愛好はイギリス国民の心情になじむものらしい．

注

1) この 'beatus ille' テーマの研究については，拙著『イギリス十八世紀小説論－言葉とイメージャリをめぐって』（開文社出版，昭和62年）六，「隠退の神話」ノート（pp.155-90）を参照していただければ幸いである．

2) *The Oxford Book of Eighteenth Century Verse*, Chosen by David Nichol Smith (1926; rpt. Oxford University Press, 1963), pp.1-6. 以下，*18th V* と略す．

なお，全篇167行を内容にしたがって便宜的に7段階に分け，行を明示した．以下，引用詩についてはほぼ同様の扱いとする．

3) *English Poetry 1700-1800, Contemporaries of Swift and Johnson*, edited by David W. Lindsay (Everyman's University Library, 1974), p.189.

この編者の注によると，この詩の背景には，Swift のパトロンであった元外交官 Sir William Temple の屋敷 Moor Park の影響があるらしい．また「わたしは妻を持たぬ故」という括弧つき一行（1.157）のために，ポムフリットは妻よりも愛人との交際

に幸福を見出す牧師だと中傷され，出世の妨げになったという有名なエピソードがある．Cf. Samuel Johnson, 'Pomfret' in *Lives of the English Poets* (1779; rpt. The World's Classics, 1952), Vol. I, pp.210-1.
4) *18th V.* pp.40-2.
5) *The Oxford Book of English Verse 1250-1918*, Chosen and Edited by Sir Arthur Quiller-Couch (1900; rpt, 1953), p.686. 以下，*English V* と略す。
6) *The New Oxford Book of Eighteenth Century Verse*, Chosen and Edited by Roger Lonsdale (Oxford University Press, 1984), pp.6-8. 以下，*New 18th V* と略す．

なお，この Philips の詩は Addison から 'the finest burlesque poem in the British language' と称されたという．Cf. Lindsay, ed. p.191. n.
7) *18th V*, pp.299-301. *New 18th V*, pp.403-4.

II　ロンドン詩

1　John Gay, 'Trivia'

　17世紀から18世紀にかけて，貴族や政治家の邸宅や庭園，またその周辺の丘，川，森，田園など自然の風光を眺望して謳う地誌的（'topographical'）な詩が流行した．Sir John Denham の『クーパーの丘』（*Cooper's Hill*, 1642）や John Dyer の『グロンガーの丘』（*Grongar Hill*, 1726）など，その典型的な作品であろう．更に『クーパーの丘』を称えたポープの『ウィンザーの森』（*Windsor Forest*, 1713）も，田園描写に歴史的回顧や文学的連想を織り込み，結局は政治的にスペイン継承戦争終結のユトレヒト条約を締結させたアン女王の平和な治世を謳歌したものであった．

　ロンドンを題材とする詩もまたこのような地誌的な詩に属すると考えてよかろう．スウィフトの「朝の情景」（'A Description of the Morning', 1709）や「都の俄雨の情景」（'A Descripfion of a City Shower', 1710），ジョンソンの『ロンドン』（*London*, 1738），ブレイクの「ロンドン」（'London', 1794）などは，多くのアンソロジーに収載されて，すでにロンドン詩の正典の位置を占めている．[1] したがって，ここではまず John Gay の『トリヴィア，あるいはロンドンの街を歩く

術』(*Trivia: or, The Art of Walking the Streets of London,* 1716)[2)] の夜の一節から始めよう.

> When Night first bids the twinkling Stars appear,
> Or with her cloudy Vest inwraps the Air,　　　　10
> Then swarms the busie Street; with Caution tread,
> Where the Shop-Windows falling threat thy Head;
> Now Lab'rers home return, and join their Strength
> To bear the tott'ring Plank, or Ladder's Length;
> Still fix thy Eyes intent upon the Throng,　　　　15
> 　　　　　　　　⋮

> まず夜が輝く星に出よと言い,
> あるいは雲の衣で空を包む頃,　　　　10
> 賑やかな通りに人が群がる, 心して歩け,
> ショーウィンドーが降りてあなたの頭を脅かす.
> 今や家路を急ぐ労働者たちが, 力を合わせ
> ぐらつく板や梯子を運ぶ.
> 目はじっと人の群れから離すでないぞ,　　　　15
> 　　　　　　　　⋮

> Forth issuing from steep Lanes, the *Collier's* Steeds　　25
> Drag the black Load; another Cart succeeds,
> Team follows Team, Crouds heap'd on Crouds appear,
> And wait impatient, 'till the Road grow clear.
> Now all the Pavement sounds with trampling Feet,
> And the mixt Hurry barricades the Street.　　　　30

Entangled here, the Waggon's lengthen'd Team
Cracks the tough Harness; Here a pond'rous Beam
Lies over-turn'd athwart; For Slaughter fed,
Here lowing Bullocks raise their horned Head.
Now Oaths grow loud, with Coaches Coaches jar, 35
And the smart Blow provokes the sturdy War;
From the high Box they whirl the Thong around,
And with the twining Lash their Shins resound:
Their Rage ferments, more dang'rous Wounds they try,
And the Blood gushes down their painful Eye. 40
And now on Foot the frowning Warriors light,
And with their pond'rous Fists renew the Fight;
Blow answers Blow, their Cheeks are smear'd with Blood,
'Till down they fall, and grappling roll in Mud.
So when two Boars, in wild *Ytene* bred, 45
Or on *Westphalia's* fatt'ning Chest-nuts fed,
Gnash their sharp Tusks, and rous'd with equal Fire,
Dispute the Reign of some luxurious Mire;
In the black Flood they wallow o'er and o'er,
'Till their arm'd Jaws distill with Foam and Gore. 50

   Where the Mob gathers, swiftly shoot along,
Nor idly mingle in the noisy Throng.
Lur'd by the silver Hilt, amid the Swarm,
The subtil Artist will thy Side disarm.

55　　Nor is thy Flaxen Wigg with Safety worn;
　　　High on the Shoulder, in the Basket born,
　　　Lurks the sly Boy; whose Hand to Rapine bred,
　　　Plucks off the curling Honours of the Head.
　　　　　　　　　　　　⋮

25　坂の路地から炭屋の馬が跳び出して
　　黒い積み荷を引きずれば，別の荷馬車がまた続く．
　　馬車また馬車が，人また人が現れて，
　　道がすくまで，いらいらと待つ．
　　今や舗道みな踏んづける足の音，
30　さまざまに慌て急いで，街を通せんぼ．
　　ここで混み合い，荷馬車の長い列
　　きつい馬具に鞭が鳴る．ここでどっしり重い車柄(え)が
　　でんぐり返って横ざまに．屠殺に飼われた
　　雄牛がここでもーと鳴き，角ある頭を持ち上げる．
35　今やまた罵り言葉が声高に，車と車が軋り合い，
　　痛烈な一撃が本格戦争を引き起こす．
　　高い御者台から革紐を振り回し
　　からまる鞭に向う脛が鳴る．
　　怒り心頭，さらに危険な果たし合い，
40　痛む目からは流血の惨．
　　そして今，渋面の戦士らはすっくと立って
　　重い拳で戦闘再開．
　　丁丁発止，かれらの頬は血に染まる，
　　どうと倒れて摑(つか)み合い，泥に転がる．
45　あたかも二匹の猪が，イテネの森で育ったか，

ウェストファリアの栗の実を餌としたか,
鋭い牙を軋らせて, 負けじと熱火にあふられて
豪奢な泥沼支配の喧嘩のようだ.
黒い流れにのたうち回り,
武装の顎から泡と血糊が滴り落ちる.　　　　　　　　　　　　50
　野次馬の集まるところ, すっと素早く身をこなし,
有象無象にも混じわるな.
銀の柄(つか)に誘われて, 群のさなかで,
掏摸(すり)の名人があなたの腰を丸裸.
亜麻の鬘(かつら)も無事とはいかぬ,　　　　　　　　　　　　55
肩のうえ高く, 籠に運ばれて,
機敏な小僧が待ち伏せし, 盗みに慣れたその手でもって,
頭の縮れた飾りをひょいと抜く.

　　　　　　　　　　　⋮

　Let not the Ballad-Singer's shrilling Strain
Amid the Swarm thy list'ning Ear detain:
Guard well the Pocket; for these *Syrens* stand
To aid the Labours of the diving Hand;　　　　　　　　　80
Confed'rate in the Cheat, they draw the Throng,
And *Cambrick* Handkerchiefs reward the Song.
But soon as Coach or Cart drives rattling on,
The Rabble part, in Shoals they backward run.
So *Jove's* loud Bolts the mingled War divide,　　　　　　85
And *Greece* and *Troy* retreats on either side.

　俗謡の歌い手の金切り声に

人込みの中，耳を傾け手間取るなかれ．
ポケットをしっかりご用心，こんな歌姫が出るわけは
80　手を突っ込む掏摸稼業を助けんがため．
詐欺のぐるになり，かれらは群衆を引き寄せて，
麻糸織りの上ハンカチが唄の報酬．
だがしかし，大型馬車か荷馬車がごろごろ来れば，
人の群れはばらばらに，群れをなして走る後すざり．
85　そのようにジュピターの大稲妻が混戦を分け，
ギリシアとトロイの双方，陣を引く．

　このように，ゲイは自ら告白するように，前述のスウィフトのロンドン詩にヒントを得て，この第3巻でロンドンの夜の街を道案内でもするがごとく，臨場感あふれた情景描写を丹念に行なったのである．

　2　Mary Robinson, 'London's Summer Morning'
　これに対し，時の皇太子（後のジョージ4世）の情婦となって社交界で浮名を流した女優メアリ・ロビンソン（1758-1800）は「ロンドン夏の朝」（'London's Summer Morning', 1794）[3] 42行を次のように歌った．

London's Summer Morning

Who has not waked to list the busy sounds
Of summer's morning, in the sultry smoke
Of noisy London? On the pavement hot
The sooty chimney-boy, with dingy face

And tattered covering, shrilly bawls his trade,
Rousing the sleepy housemaid. At the door
The milk-pail rattles, and the tinkling bell
Proclaims the dustman's office; while the street
Is lost in clouds impervious. Now begins
The din of hackney-coaches, waggons, carts; 10
While tinmen's shops, and noisy trunk-makers,
Knife-grinders, coopers, squeaking cork-cutters,
Fruit-barrows, and the hunger-giving cries
Of vegetable-vendors, fill the air.
Now every shop displays its varied trade,
And the fresh-sprinkled pavement cools the feet
Of early walkers. At the private door
The ruddy housemaid twirls the busy mop,
Annoying the smart 'prentice, or neat girl,
Tripping with band-box lightly. Now the sun 20
Darts burning splendour on the glittering pane,
Save where the canvas awning throws a shade
On the gay merchandise. Now, spruce and trim,
In shops (where beauty smiles with industry)
Sits the smart damsel; while the passenger
Peeps through the window, watching every charm.
Now pastry dainties catch the eye minute
Of humming insects, while the limy snare
Waits to enthral them. Now the lamp-lighter
Mounts the tall ladder, nimbly vent'rous, 30

To trim the half-filled lamps, while at his feet
The pot-boy yells discordant! All along
The sultry pavement, the old-clothes-man cries
In tone monotonous, and sidelong views
The area for his traffic: now the bag
Is slyly opened, and the half-worn suit
(Sometimes the pilfered treasure of the base
Domestic spoiler), for one half its worth,
Sinks in the green abyss. The porter now
40 Bears his huge load along the burning way;
And the poor poet wakes from busy dreams,
To paint the summer morning.

(Wr. *c.* 1794; pub. 1806)

目覚めれば誰しも耳にせわしない音
夏の朝の,暑苦しい煙の中
騒々しい都ロンドンの.熱い舗道で
煤だらけの煙突掃除の少年が,薄黒い顔に
よれよれの服,金切声で商売わめき立て,
眠い女中を呼び起こす.戸口では
牛乳桶がカタカタと,チリンチリンと鈴の音が
ごみ収集人の仕事のお触れ,だが街は
濁った霧に消えたまま.今や始まる
10 喧騒は,四輪馬車に荷車,手押し.
一方で,ブリキ店やら騒々しいトランク屋,
刃物の研ぎ屋に桶屋,キーキー鳴らすコルク切り,

果物車，空き腹泣かせの物売り声は
野菜売り，こういう音が空一杯．
今や店は皆とりどりの品を陳列し，
水撒きたての舗道では足も涼しげ
早朝歩く人たちは．個人個人の戸口では
赤ら顔の姐ちゃんがせわしくモップを振り回し，
困るは粋な徒弟どん，また小綺麗な娘さん
帽子箱抱えてチョコマカ歩くため．今や太陽が 20
燃える光をギラギラ窓に，
日除けの天幕だけは別，
派手な商品に影落とす．今や，小ざっぱり，
店の中（美女いそいそと微笑む所）
粋な乙女が陣取ると，通行人は
窓覗き，どんな魅力も見逃さぬ．
今やパイの珍味が捕らえる小さな目
ぶんぶん唸る昆虫の．だが一方，鳥もち塗った罠により，
虜(とりこ)にするのを待つ仕掛け．今やガス灯の点灯夫
高い梯子に上がっては，危ない仕事を敏捷に， 30
半ば灯った芯を切る．だが，その足許で
酒屋の小僧が耳障りなわめき声．また
蒸し暑い舗道では，古着屋が声あげる
口調は単調，そして流し目に見る
商売の縄張り．今や袋が
そっと開かれて，着古しの服
（時には盗品の宝物，卑しい
押し込み強盗の），値打ちの半分で

三百代言の緑のカバンの底に沈みゆく．今や担ぎ屋が
でっかい重荷を運びゆく，焼けつく道に沿いながら．
そこでようやくへぼ詩人，せわしい夢から目を覚まし，
描こうとする夏の朝．

　この風物詩は18世紀も終わりに近いが，朝と夜との差，春
と夏との季節の差はあれ，世紀初頭のスウィフトやゲイが歌っ
たロンドン風景とさして変わるところがない．相も変わらずい
かにもエネルギーと喧騒に溢れた庶民の暮らしぶり，雑踏の賑
わいが描かれている．

3　Anonymous, 'A Description of the Spring in London'

　最後にもう一つ，読み人知らずの風物詩「ロンドン春景色」
('A Description of the Spring in London', 1754)[4] を取り上
げておこう．

A DESCRIPTION OF THE SPRING IN LONDON

Now new-vamped silks the mercer's window shows,
And his spruce 'prentice wears his Sunday clothes;
His annual suit with nicest taste renewed,
The reigning cut and colour still pursued.
　　The barrow now, with oranges a score,
Driv'n by at once a gamester and a whore,
No longer gulls the stripling of his pence,

Who learns that poverty is nurse to sense.
Much-injured trader whom the law pursues,
The law which winked and beckoned to the Jews,   10
Why should the beadle drive thee from the street?
To sell is always a pretence to cheat.

 'Large stewing-oysters!', in a deep'ning groan,
No more resounds, not 'Mussels!' shriller tone;
Sev'n days to labour now is held no crime,   15
And Moll 'New Mack'rel!' screams in sermon-time.

 In ruddy bunches radishes are spread,
And Nan with choice-picked salad loads her head.

 Now, in the suburb window, Christmas green,
The bays and holly are no longer seen,   20
But sprigs of garden-mint in vials grow,
And gathered laylocks perish as they blow.

 The truant schoolboy now at eve we meet,
Fatigued and sweating throught the crowded street,
His shoes embrowned at once with dust and clay,   25
With whitethorn loaded, which he takes for May:
Round his flapped hat in rings the cowslips twine,
Or in cleft osiers form a golden line.

⋮

In gay Vauxhall now saunter beaux and belles,   35
And happier cits resort to Sadler's Wells.

A<small>NON</small>., 1754

いま，手直しの絹物が呉服屋の窓辺を飾り，
　　　粋な徒弟が一張羅の晴着をつける．
　　　年一度の服は好みを凝らして縫い直し，
　　　裁ち方や色合いも時の流行．
5　　　　手押し車は今，オレンジを山と載せ，
　　　賭博好きと娼婦とに追い立てられて，
　　　もはや小僧を騙して小金も取れぬ，
　　　貧乏は分別の乳母と承知ゆえ．
　　　法に追われる損な商人，
10　　ユダヤ人には目くばせ手招きの法なのに，
　　　小役人どうしてお前を街から追い立てる？
　　　売るとはきまって騙す口実．
　　　　'シチューになる大牡蛎(かき)だよ!' の太い唸り声は
　　　もやは響かぬ．さらに甲高い'ムール貝'の声の調子も．
15　　いま７日働くことも罪とはならぬ．
　　　そこでモル'活きた鯖だよ!' の金切り声は説教の最中(さなか)．
　　　　大根が赤く束ねて拡げられ，
　　　ナンは選り抜き野菜を頭に載せる．
　　　　いま，郊外の窓辺には，クリスマスの飾りの
20　　月桂樹や柊(ひいらぎ)はもう見られない，
　　　だが庭の薄荷の小枝が瓶に活けられ，
　　　摘んできたライラックは咲きながら枯れる．
　　　　いま夕べ怠け坊主の児童に会うと，
　　　人込みの街に疲れて汗をかき，
25　　靴は埃と土で茶色になって，
　　　サンザシを背負い，五月の祭に備え，

ぺちゃんこ帽子の回りには九輪桜が巻きついて，
　　　また裂けた柳で金色のひも作り．

⋮

　　　賑やかなヴォクソールでは，いま，そぞろ歩きの美男美女，　35
　　　もっと幸せな市民らはサドラーズウェルズへ繰り出して
　　　行く．

　この 18 世紀半ばの春景色の詩でも，このように商家とその手代，ロンドン名物の呼び売り，露天商，腕白坊主など，これまでのロンドン詩と大同小異の風景であろう．例の「ロンドンに飽いたら，人生に飽いたも同然だ」というジョンソン博士の有名な言葉があるように，18 世紀の首都ロンドンを歌った詩がいくら出てきても不思議ではあるまい．

注

1) 拙著『スウィフトの詩』(九州大学出版会，1993)，二　スウィフトのロンドン詩二篇，pp.75-113 参照．

2) Book III 'Of Walking the Streets by Night', ll. 9-15: 25-58; 77-86, in Lindsay, ed., pp.32-4.

3) *Eighteenth-Century Women Poets: An Oxford Anthology*, ed. Roger Lonsdale (Oxford University Press, 1989), pp.472-3. 以下このアンソロジーは *18th WP* と略す．

4) *The Oxford Book of London* (Oxford University Press, 1996), ed. Paul Bailey, pp.78-9.

III 風刺の詩

1 Anon., 'The Vicar of Bray'

　風刺の全盛時代ともいうべき18世紀から,もはやポープやジョンソンは別として,風刺の詩を省くわけにはいくまい.元来,風刺は単なる皮肉や中傷ではなく,理想主義的な精神を内に秘めていて,社会や人間の悪徳や愚行を,辛辣にか寛容にか,笑いを通して改善,矯正しようとするものであってみれば,昔から聖職者,弁護士,医者などの持つ権威,偽善,腐敗や堕落が批判の対象となりやすかった.

　ここではまず匿名氏の「ブレイの牧師」(1734)[1] から始めよう.

Anon

THE VICAR OF BRAY

In CHARLES the Second's Golden Days
　　When Loyalty no Harm meant,
A furious High Churchman I was,
　　And so I got Preferment;
Unto my Flock daily preach'd

Ⅲ　風刺の詩　　　　　　　　　　　　33

 Kings were by God appointed,
And damn'd was he, that durst resist,
 Or touch the Lord's Anointed.

Chor. *That this is Law, I will maintain*
 Unto my dying Day, Sir,   10
That whatsoever King shall reign,
 I will be Vicar of Bray, *Sir.*

チャールズ2世の黄金の世は
忠義が損にはならぬ時,
わたしゃ激しい高教会派,
それで出世したもんだ.
信者に毎日説いたのは   5
王とは神の任命で,
地獄に行くのは反抗者,
または聖別の王に手をかける者.

コーラス．これが掟と，言いまする
命の終わるその日まで，はいあなた,   10
どんな王様の統治でも,
わたしゃブレイの坊さまよ，はいあなた.

When Royal J<small>AMES</small> possess'd the Crown,
 And Pop'ry grew in Fashion,
The penal Laws I hooted down,   15

34

  And read the Declaration;
 The Church of *Rome* I found would fit,
  Full well my Constitution,
 And had become a Jesuit,
20 But for the Revolution.

That this is law, I will maintain, &c.

 ジェイムズ王が王冠持って,
 カトリックが流行した頃は,
15 審査律など嘲って,
 寛容宣言を読みました.
 ローマの教会どうやらぴったり
 わたしの性によく合って,
 イエズス会士になったでしょう,
20 名誉革命さえなかったら.

これが掟と, 言いまする, 等々.

 When W<small>ILLIAM</small> our Deliverer came,
  To heal tha Nations Grievance,
 I turn'd the Cat in Pan again,
25 And swore to him Allegiance;
 Old Principles I did revoke,
  Set Conscience at a distance;
 Passive Obedience was a Joke,

Ⅲ　風刺の詩　　　　　　　　　　35

A Jest was Non-resistance.

That this is Law, I will maintain, &c.　　　　　　30

ウィリアム解放者がお出ましの時は,
国の苦悩を癒すとて,
わたしゃまたまた寝返って,
忠義の誓いを立てました.　　　　　　　　　25
昔の主義は取り消して,
良心はちょっと遠ざけた.
臣従拒否なんか笑い草,
無抵抗こそシャレたこと.

これが掟と, 言いまする, 等々.　　　　　　　30

When Gracious Aɴɴ became our Queen,
　The Church of *Englands* Glory,
Another Face of Things were seen,
　And I became a Tory;
Occasional Conformest base　　　　　　　35
　I damn'd, and such Evasion,
And swore the Church wou'd ruin'd be
　From such Prevarication.

That this is Law, I will maintain, &c.

徳高きアンがわれらの女王，
国教会の栄光となって，
世情の様子が変わってくると，
トーリー保守に鞍替えた．
35 日和見信者を卑劣だと
罵った，それにあんな逃げ口上，
断言もした，教会は破滅だと
あんな言い逃れが通るなら．

これが掟と，言いまする，等々．

40 When GEORGE in Pudding-time came o'er,
    And moderate Men look'd big, Sir.
My principles I chang'd once more,
    And so became a Whig, Sir;
And thus Preferment I procur'd
45   From our great Faith's Defender,
And every now and then abjur'd
    The Pope and the Pretender.

That this is Law, I will maintain, &c.

40 ジョージが好機と渡来して，
温和な男が偉く見え，はいあなた，
わたしゃもう一度主義変えて，
それでホイッグ党員になったのさぁー．

Ⅲ　風刺の詩　　　　　　　　　　37

こうして出世を手に入れた
われらの偉い信仰擁護のお方から. 45
そして時々捨てました
教皇殿や老僧王.

これが掟と, 言いまする, 等々.

Th' Illustrious House of *Hanover*,
　　And Protestant Succession, 50
To these I lustily will swear
　　While they can keep Possession,
And in my Faith and Loyalty
　　I never once will falter,
And G<small>EORGE</small> my lawful King shall be, 55
　　Unless the Times shall alter.

That this is Law, I will maintain
　　Unto my dying Day, Sir.
That whatsoever King shall reign,
　　I will be Vicar of Bray, Sir. 60

栄えある王朝ハノーヴァー,
プロテスタントの継承で, 50
わたしゃ心底誓います
かれらの領有続く間は,
信仰, 忠誠どちらでも

一度たりとも揺らぎません,
55　ジョージがわたしの正しい王で,
　　　時勢が変われば別だけど.

　　　これが掟と, 言いまする
　　　命終わるその日まで, はいあなた.
　　　どんな王様の統治でも,
60　わたしゃブレイの坊さまよ, はいあなた.

　このように,「審査律」('the Test Acts', 1673, 1678),「寛容の宣言」('the Declaration of Indulgence', 1688),「宣誓拒否者」('Non-jurors', 1689),「便宜的国教遵奉」('Occasional Conformity', 1711) など, さまざまな法令や動きを織り込んで, さながら王政復古から18世紀前半までの宗教史の変遷をなぞるかのように, 当時の宗教界の無節操ぶりの一端が実に赤裸々に暴露されている. すなわち, カトリックへの憧れを秘めたチャールズ2世から, 公然とカトリック教徒を名乗ったジェイムズ2世を経て, ほどなくオレンジ公ウィリアムとメアリ女王の名誉革命, 続くアン女王の後, ハノーヴァー王朝のジョージ1世に至る治世の間, カトリックからプロテスタントへ, 政教一体の激動の時世の中を巧みに遊泳して, 身の保全と出世を計った風見鶏牧師の日和見主義を痛烈に風刺したものである.

　序に, 付言しておこう. 各連のあとコーラスが繰り返されるうちに, バラッドのリフレインよろしく, 風刺的効果が漸増して, 時の宗教界に対する名も無き庶民の嘲弄か怨嗟の感情が増幅される仕掛けになっている.

III 風刺の詩

2 John Collier, 'The Pluralist and Old Soldier'

次はジョン・コリア (1708-86) の対話「兼領牧師と老兵」
(1763)[2] 30行を読んでみよう.

The Pluralist and Old Soldier

A SOLDIER maimed and in the beggars' list
Did thus address a well-fed pluralist:
Sol. At Guadeloupe my leg and thigh I lost,
　No pension have I, though its right I boast;
　Your reverence, please some charity bestow,
　Heav'n will pay double—when you're there, you know.
Plu. Heav'n pay me double! Vagrant—know that I
　Ne'er give to strollers, they're so apt to lie:
　Your parish and some work would you become,
　So haste away—or constable's your doom.　　　　10
Sol. May't please your reverence, hear my case, and then
　You'll say I'm poorer than the most of men:
　When Marlbro siegèd Lisle, I first drew breath,
　And there my father met untimely death;
　My mother followed, of a broken heart,
　So I've no friend or parish, for my part.
Plu. I say, begone.
　　　　　　—With that, he loudly knocks,

40

>   And Timber-toe begins to smell the stocks.
>   Away he stumps—but, in a rood or two,
> 20 He cleared his weasand and his thoughts broke through:
>   *Sol.* This 'tis to beg of those who sometimes preach
>   Calm charity, and ev'ry virtue teach;
>   But their disguise to common sense is thin:
>   A pocket buttoned—hypocrite within.
>   Send me, kind heav'n, the well-tanned captain's face,
>   Who gives me twelvepence and a curse, with grace;
>   But let me not, in house or lane or street,
>   These treble-pensioned parsons ever meet;
>   And when I die, may I still numbered be
> 30   With the rough soldier, to eternity.
>
>   (1763)

不具になった乞食名簿の老兵が
太った坊さまに言いました．
兵．グァドループで脚と腿をやられました．
　　年金はありません．権利は十分と思うのですが．
　　牧師さま，どうか少々お恵みを，
　　神が倍してお返しなさる ── 往生されたそのときは，
　　です．
牧．神が倍してお返し，と！　浮浪者め ── 知るがよい
　　宿無しに恵む金はない，奴等はたいてい嘘つきだ．

Ⅲ　風刺の詩

　　教区に帰って仕事をするのが一番だ．
　　とっとと失せろ── さもなきゃお巡りに渡すまで．
兵．畏れながら牧師さま，事情を聞いておくんなさい，そうすりゃ
　　人並みはずれて哀れな男と言いなすろう．
　　モールバラがリールを攻めた頃，わたしゃようやく
　　生まれたわけで．
　　ところが親父はそこで名誉の戦死，
　　母も続いて，悲嘆のあまり，
　　それで身内も教区もないのです，手前には．
牧．去れ，と言うに．
　　　　　　── それを聞き，老兵心臓が高鳴って，
義足が晒しの刑を感づいて
足取り重く出て行くが── 数メートルも行かぬうち，
咳払いをひとつして，胸の想いを吐き出した．
兵．物を乞うとこのざまだ，時折りの説教で
　　やさしい愛とか徳を教える人なのに．
　　分別の見せかけも透けている．
　　懐にはボタンがかかり── 内は偽善者．
　　送って下され，優しい神よ，日焼けした隊長の顔を，
　　彼なら大枚と舌打ちを，あっさり呉れる，
　　だが金輪際，家でも路でも通りでも
　　多重年金坊主に逢うのはご免．
　　死んだら，それでも入れますように
　　荒くれ兵士と天国へ．

この対話詩もまた世俗化した宗教界の偽善的な聖職者に対する風刺であることに変わりはない.

3 Soame Jenyns, 'The Modern Fine Gentleman' and 'The Modern Fine Lady'

最後に, 18世紀の粋な当世風の紳士淑女に登場してもらおう. まずソウム・ジェニンズ (1704-87) の「当世風紳士」(1746)[3] の一節から始めたい.

from *The Modern Fine Gentleman*

After the Grand Tour

  Just broke from school, pert, impudent, and raw,
  Expert in Latin, more expert in taw,
  His Honour posts o'er Italy and France,
  Measures St. Peter's dome, and learns to dance.
5 Thence, having quick through various countries flown,
  Gleaned all their follies, and exposed his own,
  He back returns, a thing so strange all o'er,
  As never ages past produced before;
  A monster of such complicated worth,
10 As no one single clime could e'er bring forth;
  Half atheist, papist, gamester, bubble, rook,
  Half fiddler, coachman, dancer, groom, and cook.
   Next, because business is now all the vogue,

III　風刺の詩　　　　　　　　　　　　　　43

And who'd be quite polite must be a rogue,
In parliament he purchases a seat,　　　　　　　　15
To make the accomplished gentleman complete.
There safe in self-sufficient impudence,
Without experience, honesty, or sense,
Unknowing in her int'rest, trade, or laws,
He vainly undertakes his country's cause:　　　　　20
Forth from his lips, prepared at all to rail,
Torrents of nonsense burst, like bottled ale,
Though shallow, muddy; brisk, though mighty dull;
Fierce without strength; o'erflowing, though not full.
　　　　bubble] dupe　　rook] cheat

ちょうど学業やめにして，生意気，不遜で未熟者，
ラテン語ができ，はじき石遊びはもっとでき，
若様イタリア，フランスを早馬で
ペテロの伽藍を見物し，それにダンスを身につける．
それから諸国を飛び歩き，　　　　　　　　　　　5
愚かな遊びはみな探り，己の恥はかき捨てる．
国に帰れば，まったくの別人に変わり果て，
いままでの世の中に例がない．
それほど混み入った値打ちの怪物だ，
国ひとつではとても産み出せぬ，　　　　　　　10
半ば無神論者でカトリック，ばくち打ちで間抜けに詐欺師，
半ばヴァイオリン弾き，御者，ダンサー，馬丁にコック．
　さて次は，今や仕事は大流行で，

上流めざせば悪党は必定,
15　議会で議員の席を買い,
完璧な教養紳士に成り澄ます.
そこで安閑, 自信過剰の横柄さ,
経験, 誠実, 分別ないくせに.
国益, 貿易, 法をわきまえず,
20　やたら天下国家を振りかざす.
口から外へ出るものは, 罵倒しようと構えるが,
たわごとの滝がほとばしる, 瓶詰めビールと同じこと,
深みはないが濁り切り, 味は抜けても泡は立つ,
強さがなくて激しくて, 一杯でなくても溢れ出る.

　このように, 大陸巡遊の旅で遊興と悪業を覚えた若殿を取り上げて, その相手たる「当世風淑女」の肖像に多少とも触れなければ, これは片手落ちというものであろう. やはり同じ作者の 'The Modern Fine Lady' (1751), 全 98 行中の一節 (ll.35-48)[4] だけでも訳出しておこう.

From *The Modern Fine Lady*

But soon th'endearments of a husband cloy,
Her soul, her frame incapable of joy:
She feels no transports in the bridal-bed,
Of which so oft sh'has heard, so much has read;
Then vexed, that she should be condemned alone
40　To seek in vain this philosophic stone,

To abler tutors she resolves t'apply,
A prostitute from curiosity:
Hence men of every sort and every size,
Impatient for Heaven's cordial drop, she tries;
The fribbling beau, the rough unwieldy clown, 45
The ruddy templar newly on the town,
The Hibernian captain of gigantic make,
The brimful parson, and th'exhausted rake.

SOAME JENYNS

　だがしかし，夫の愛撫に直ぐに飽き,
心も体も喜べぬ．
初夜の床でも夢中になれぬ,
話しに聞いた，読みもしたのに．
苛立ち挙句は，孤独の地獄,
いたずらに賢者の石を探す羽目, 40
腕きき導師に当たって砕けと
好奇心から売笑婦．
それから男を手当り次第,
天の甘露をあれこれ試す．
軽薄な伊達男，荒くれの手に負えぬ無骨者, 45
血色のよい法学生，夜遊びの新顔で,
アイルランドの隊長はいかつい造りの大男,
はち切れそうなお坊さま，憔悴し切った遊蕩児．

このような風刺的スケッチを通してでも，王政復古時代から

18世紀前半にかけて, 爛熟した上流社会の一断面が窺えよう. いや, Hogarth の風俗画「当世風結婚」('Marriage à la Mode', 1745) などを篤と眺めるのが早道かもしれない.

注

1) James Kinsley and James T. Boulton, eds., *English Satiric Poetry: Dryden to Byron* (Edward Arnold, 1966), pp.47-50. なお, 次のアンソロジーにも収録されているが, テキストに多少の違いがある. *The Oxford Book of Satirical Verse*, ed. Geoffrey Grigson (1980; Oxford Univ. Press paperback, 1983), pp.158-60. 以下, *Satirical V* と略.
2) *New 18th V*, p.511.
3) *Satirical V*, p.188. なお, Jeremy Collier の *A Short View of the Immorality and Profaneness of the English Stage* (1698) には 'A fine Gentleman' を痛烈に非難した一節がある. Cf. J. E. Spingarn, ed., *Critical Essays of the Seventeenth Century,* Vol.III, 1685−1700 (Oxford Univ. Press, 1908; rpt. 1957), pp.255-6.
4) *The Penguin Book of Eighteenth Century English Verse*, edited and introduced by Dennis Davison (Penguin Books, 1973), p.21.

IV 賛美歌

　端的に言えば，賛美歌は作者の敬虔な想いを述べた宗教詩にほかなるまい．事実，賛美歌の中には，その思想，感情，構造，韻律，詞藻いずれの点においても，優れた詩として18世紀英詩の一翼を担うに足るものがある．[1]

　Cowper や Smart，また Addison や Steele までも宗教詩や賛美歌を書いているが，[2] とりわけこの時期の賛美歌の第一人者として，ジョンソン博士がその清純な信仰を推賞した非国教徒 Isaac Watts (1674-1748)[3]，あるいは数千もの夥しい賛美歌を作った Charles Wesley (1707-88) の名を挙げなくてはならない．

1　Isaac Watts, 'The Day of Judgement'

　まずウォッツ (1674−1748) の「裁きの日」[4]の頌歌，サッポー風英詩体の試みから始めよう．

The Day of Judgment

An Ode

Attempted in English Sapphick

WHEN the fierce Northwind with his airy Forces
Rears up the *Baltick* to a foaming Fury;
And the red Lightning with a Storm of Hail comes
       Rushing amain down,

How the poor Sailors stand amaz'd and tremble!
While the hoarse Thunder like a bloody Trumpet
Roars a loud Onset to the gaping Waters
       Quick to devour them.

Such shall the Noise be, and the wild Disorder,
(If things Eternal may be like these Earthly)
Such the dire Terror when the great Archangel
       Shakes the Creation;

荒れ狂う北風が大気の軍勢を引き連れ
バルト海を泡立つ憤怒へと持ち上げて,
赤い稲妻が雹の嵐とともに
      まっしぐらに襲いかかる,

哀れな船乗りどもがいかに呆然と立ちつくし震えることか!
嗄れ声の雷が殺伐たるトランペットのごとく
大口を開ける大波に大音声の突撃を呼ぶとき
      素早く彼等を呑み込めと.

かくあらん, その喧騒と激しき混乱は,

IV 賛美歌

(もし永遠なるものがこれら地上のもののごとくなら)
極度の恐怖もかくあらん，大いなる大天使が
    森羅万象を揺り動かすときは．

Tears the strong Pillars of the Vault of Heaven,
Breaks up old Marble the Repose of Princes;
See the Graves open, and the Bones arising,
    Flames all around 'em.

Hark the shrill Outcries of the guilty Wretches!
Lively bright Horror and amazing Anguish
Stare thro' their Eye-lids, while the living Worm lies
    Gnawing within them.

Thoughts like old Vultures prey upon their Heart-strings,
And the Smart twinges, when their Eye beholds the
Lofty Judge frowning, and a Flood of Vengeance
    Rolling afore him.

蒼穹の強き柱を引き裂き，
王侯の憩たる古びた大理石の館を破壊する．
見よ墓が口を開き，骨が起き上がり，
    あたり一帯を焔に包む．

罪深き哀れなる者どもの甲高い叫び声を聴け！

真に迫る鮮やかな戦慄と驚くべき苦悶が
彼等の瞼を貫く，生きた蛆(うじ)が横たわり
      彼等の体を蝕むとき．

くさぐさの想いが老いたる禿鷹のごとく彼等の玉の緒を
餌食にし
刺すような痛みがうずく，彼等の目に見えるとき
高御座(たかみくら)の裁き手の渋面が，復讐の上げ潮が
      御前(みまえ)に逆巻くときに．

Hopeless Immortals! how they scream and shiver
While Devils push them to the Pit wide yawning
Hideous and gloomy, to receive them headlong
      Down to the Centre.

Stop here my Fancy: (all away ye horrid
Doleful Ideas) come arise to *Jesus,*
How he sits God-like! and the Saints around him
      Thron'd, yet adoring!

O may I sit there when he comes Triumphant
Dooming the Nations: then ascend to Glory,
While our *Hosannahs* all along the Passage
      Shout the Redeemer.
       Horae Lyricae, 1706

IV 賛美歌

望みなき不死の人々よ！ 彼等はいかに絶叫し震えおのの
くことか
悪魔らに大口を開けた奈落へと押しやられ
忌まわしき陰鬱，真逆さまに
      地獄の底へと落ちるとき．

わが幻想よ，ここにて止まれ，（立ち去れ汝等恐ろしき
陰鬱なる想念よ）いざイエスのもとに立ち来たれ，
神々しくも座し給う！ イエスを囲む聖者らも
      席につき，崇めたてまつる！

ああ我もかしこに座りたし，勝利のイエスの再臨で，
諸国の民が裁かれる！ そうして栄光の座へ昇りたし，
我等の賛美の歌がその道筋で
      贖いの主を称えるときに．

このように，この「最後の審判の日」の歌は，単に神やキリストを称えるだけの月並みな賛美歌と違い，キリストの再臨を前にしたキリスト者の内なる心に描く地獄図にほかならず，罪と信仰への深い畏怖を喚起してやまない．キリスト教徒ならずとも，この「恐怖の賛美歌」（'atrocity hymns'）の迫力に圧倒されるのではあるまいか．

 もう一つ同じ作者の「キリスト磔刑の死」（'Crucifixion to the World by the Cross of Christ'）[5]を読もう．

*Crucifixion to the World by the Cross
of Christ*

WHEN I survey the wond'rous Cross
On which the Prince of Glory dy'd,
My richest Gain I count but Loss,
And pour Contempt on all my Pride.

Forbid it, Lord, that I should boast
Save in the Death of *Christ* my God;
All the vain things that charm me most,
I sacrifice them to his Blood.

See from his Head, his Hands, his Feet,
Sorrow and Love flow mingled down;
Did e'er such Love and Sorrow meet?
Or Thorns compose so rich a Crown?

His dying Crimson like a Robe
Spreads o'er his Body on the Tree,
Then am I dead to all the Globe,
And all the Globe is dead to me.

Were the whole Realm of Nature mine,
That were a Present far too small;
Love so amazing, so divine
Demands my Soul, my Life, my All.

IV 賛美歌

Hymns and Spiritual Songs, 1707

あの驚くべき十字架をじっと見詰めると
その上で栄光の君は死に就かれたのだが,
わたしの最大の利得すら唯の損失と思われ,
わたしの驕慢に侮蔑を注ぐ.

禁じ給え, 主よ, わたしが誇ることを　　　　　　　　　5
わたしの神キリストの死においてのほかは.
わたしをこの上なく魅了する空なる物事はみな,
キリストの血に生贄として供えよう.

見よキリストの頭から, 両手から, 両足から,
悲しみと愛が混じり流れ落ちるのを.　　　　　　　　　10
今迄にこのような愛と悲しみが出会ったことがあっただ
ろうか?
あるいは茨がこのように見事な冠を作ったことが.

死に染まる深紅の色が緩やかな上衣のように
十字架のキリストの体にひろがる.
その時わたしは全世界に対して死に,　　　　　　　　　15
そして全世界はわたしに対して死ぬる.

たとえ自然界すべてがわたしのものとなっても,
それは誠に小さ過ぎる贈り物だろう.
それほど驚嘆すべき, それほど神々しい愛が,

20 　わたしの魂を，わたしの命を，わたしのすべてを求める
　　のだ．

　これは前作と対照的に，賛美歌調の韻律を奏でながら，静か
にキリストの十字架上の死による贖罪の意義を説いたのである．
ここで謳われた限りない愛と深い悲しみの融け合ったキリスト
の顔には，フランスの画家ルオー（Georges Rouault, 1871-
1958）の「キリスト」を重ね合わせたくなる．この賛美歌も
また優れた宗教詩として，人の心に惻々と訴えかけてくるもの
がある．

　このほかこの賛美歌作者には，子供たちのために書かれた
「怠惰と悪戯を戒めて」（'Against Idleness and Mischief',
1715）とか「無精者」（'The Sluggard', 1715）というような
教訓詩があるが，これらは作者の余技として言及するに止めよ
う．

　2 Charles Wesley, 'Resurrection'
　もう一人の賛美歌作者，ウェズレー兄弟の弟 Charles の賛美
歌から2篇を引こう．まずは「復活」（'Resurrection'）[6] から
始める．

C. Wesley, 1707-88.

1　LOVE'S redeeming work is done;
　　Fought the fight, the battle won:
　　Lo, our Sun's eclipse is o'er!
　　Lo, he sets in blood no more!

IV　賛美歌　　　　　　　　55

2 Vain the stone, the watch, the seal,
　Christ has burst the gates of hell;
　Death in vain forbids his rise;
　Christ has opened Paradise.

3 Lives again our glorious King;
　Where, O Death, is now thy sting?
　Dying once, he all doth save;
　Where thy victory, O grave?

4 Soar we now where Christ has led,
　Following our exalted Head;
　Made like him, like him we rise;
　Ours the cross, the grave, the skies.

5 Hail the Lord of earth and heaven!
　Praise to thee by both be given:
　Thee we greet triumphant now;
　Hail, the Resurrection thou!

1　愛の贖いの業(わざ)は終わりぬ，
　戦いをたたかい，戦闘に勝てり．
　見よ，我等の太陽の蝕は過ぎゆけり！
　見よ，我等の太陽はもはや血に沈むことなし！

2　空しきは石，見張り，封印，

キリストは地獄の門を破りぬ．
　　　死は主の昇天を停めるも甲斐なし，
　　　キリストは天国を開けり．

3　再び蘇る栄光の王，
　　　おお死よ，汝の牙は今いずこにありや？
　　　一度は死して，王はすべてを救う．
　　　汝の勝利はいずこ，おお墓よ？

4　我等は今キリストの導き給いし所に昇る，
　　　我等の高貴な御顔に従い，
　　　かれの如く作られ，かれの如く我等は昇る，
　　　我等のもの，十字架，墓，御空は．

5　地と天の主よ万歳！
　　　天地(あめつち)によって主が讃えられんことを，
　　　主を我等はいま勝ち誇りて迎う．
　　　万歳，なんじ復活よ！

　もう一つ同じ作者の「さあ来たれ，悩めるわが仲間たちよ」('Come on, my Partners in Distress', 1749)[7] を紹介しておこう．

Come on, my partners in distress
1
Come on, my partners in distress,

IV 賛美歌

My comrades through the wilderness,
　　Who still your bodies feel;
Awhile forget your griefs and fears,
And look beyond this vale of tears　　　　　　　5
　　To that celestial hill.

2

Beyond the bounds of time and space
Look forward to that heavenly place,
　　The saints' secure abode;
On faith's strong eagle pinions rise,　　　　　　10
And force your passage to the skies,
　　And scale the mount of God.

3

Who suffer with our Master here,
We shall before his face appear,
　　And by his side sit down;　　　　　　　　　15
To patient faith the prize is sure,
And all that to the end endure
　　The cross, shall wear the crown.

1

さあ来たれ，悩めるわが仲間たちよ，
荒野を通るわが同志たちよ，
あなたの肉体を常に感じ，

時に悲しみや恐れを忘れて，
この涙の谷のかなたに
あのシオンの丘を仰ぐ人たちよ．

2

時間と空間の境を越えて
あの天上の地を俟ち望め，
聖者らの安らう住処．
信仰の強き鷲の翼にて昇り，
天空へ押し分けて進み，
神の山によじ登れ．

3

ここにて我等の主とともに悩み，
我等はその御顔の前に現れ，
その傍に座ろう．
忍耐強き信仰に褒美は確か，
終わりまで十字架に耐え抜く者は皆
いのちの冠をいただくであろう．

4

Thrice blessed bliss-inspiring hope!
It lifts the fainting spirits up,
　It brings to life the dead;
Our conflicts here shall soon be past,
And you and I ascend at last

Triumphant with our head.

5

That great mysterious Deity 25
We soon with open face shall see;
   The beatific sight
Shall fill heaven's sounding courts with praise,
And wide diffuse the golden blaze
   Of everlasting light. 30

4

幾重にも祝福された至福の希望よ!
それは挫ける心を持ち上げ, 20
死者たちを蘇らせる.
我等の此の世の争いは直ぐに過ぎ去り,
あなた方と私は遂に昇る
キリストと共に意気揚々と.

5

あの大いなる不可思議の神を 25
我等は目を見開いて見るだろう.
天国の至福に輝く栄光が
その王宮を賞賛で鳴り響かせ,
あまねく放つであろう, 黄金の炎を
永遠の光の. 30

60

6

The Father shining on his throne,
The glorious, co-eternal Son,
　The Spirit, one and seven,
Conspire our rapture to complete,
35　And lo! we fall before his feet,
　And silence heightens heaven.

7

In hope of that ecstatic pause,
Jesu, we now sustain the cross,
　And at thy footstool fall,
40　Till thou our hidden life reveal,
Till thou our ravished spirits fill,
　And God is all in all.

1749

6

御座(みくら)に輝く父なる神と,
燦然と永久(とわ)に在る子と,
霊, 一つと七つが,
相計りて我等の歓喜を全きものとする,
35　そして見よ, 我等は主の御前に伏し,
そして静寂が天を高める.

7

あの恍惚の憩いを待ち望み,

イエスよ, いま我等は十字架を支え,

あなたの足台に伏す,

あなたが我等の隠れた命を顕わすまで,

あなたが我等の忘我の霊を満たすまで,

そして神は掛け替えのない存在となる.

終わりに, 一言蛇足を加えるならば, このように, 一般信徒の礼拝と慰励のための平易な宗教歌唱であれ, 超絶者としての神や救世主を称える荘重な文体の詩歌であれ, 18世紀はイギリスにおける賛美歌全盛時代をひらいたわけであった.

注

1) Cf. Donald Davie, *The Eighteenth Century Hymn in England* (Cambridge University Press, 1993)

2) *The Spectator*, Nos. 441; 453; 465; 489; 513. 特に Addison (1672-1719) には, 「もろもろの天は神の栄光をあらわし, 穹蒼(おほそら)はその御手のわざを示す」に始まる旧約聖書「詩篇」(第19編1～4節) に基づいて, その翻案とも読める3連24行の賛美歌がある. *The Spectator*, No.465 (Saturday, September 20, 1712) 参照.

3) Dr. Johnson, 'Watts' in *Lives of the English Poets* (*The World's Classics*, Vol.II; rpt. 1956). pp.360-7.

4) *18th V.* pp.47-8

5) Ibid., p.53.

6) *The English Hymnal* (1906; rpt. Oxford University Press, 1972), No.135, pp.121-2.

7) Margaret Ferguson, Mary Jo Salter, Jon Stallworthy, eds., *The Norton Anthology of Poetry,* Fourth Edition (1970; rpt. W. W. Norton & Company, Inc., 1996), pp.591-2.

V　ロマン詩

1　Anne Finch, Countess of Winchilsea, 'A Nocturnal Reverie'

18世紀初頭を飾るロマン詩としては，正典に属するものかもしれないが，まず第一にやはりウィンチルシー伯爵夫人アン・フィンチ (1661-1720) の名篇「夜の夢想」(1709) 50行を挙げぬわけにはいくまい．なにしろ Wordsworth が，この詩と Pope の *The Windsor Forest* (1713) の一，二か所を除けば，Milton の *Paradise Lost* (1667) から Thomson の *The Seasons* (1730) の間の英詩は清新な外的自然のイメージを1行として含んでいない，と激賞したものである．[1]

18世紀英詩の主流が，Pope や Johnson に代表されるような都市や応接間を題材にした風刺詩から始まって，次第に Young, Blair, Gray, Collins, Cowper, Burns たち，文学史のいわゆる 'Pre-Romantics' によって夕暮や夜や墓場，また田舎や農村の風景が盛んに描かれるようになった．このような動向を振り返ってみると，この「夜の夢想」はロマン詩の先鞭をつけたのではなかろうか．以下，その自然描写を見よう．

A NOCTURNAL REVERIE[2]

In such a Night, when every louder Wind
Is to its distant Cavern safe confin'd;
And only gentle Zephyr fans his Wings,
And lonely Philomel, still waking, sings;
Or from some Tree, fam'd for the Owl's Delight,
She, hollowing clear, directs the Wand'rer right:
In such a Night, when passing Clouds give place,
Or thinly vail the Heav'ns mysterious Face;
When in some River, overhung with Green,
The waving Moon and trembling Leaves are seen;
When freshen'd Grass now bears it self upright,
And makes cool Banks to pleasing Rest invite,
Whence springs the Woodbind, and the Bramble-Rose,
And where the sleepy Cowslip shelter'd grows;
Whilst now a paler Hue the Foxglove takes,
Yet checquers still with Red the dusky brakes:
When scatter'd Glow-worms, but in Twilight fine,
Shew trivial Beauties watch their Hour to shine;
Whilst Salisb'ry stands the Test of every Light,
In perfect Charms, and perfect Virtue bright:
When Odours, which declin'd repelling Day,
Thro' temp'rate Air uninterrupted stray;
When darken'd Groves their softest Shadows wear,

And falling Waters we distinctly hear;
When thro' the Gloom more venerable shows 25
Some ancient Fabrick, awful in Repose,
While Sunburnt Hills their swarthy Looks conceal,
And swelling Haycocks thicken up the Vale:
When the loos'd Horse now, as his Pasture leads,
Comes slowly grazing thro' th' adjoining Meads, 30
Whose stealing Pace, and lengthen'd Shade we fear,
Till torn up Forage in his Teeth we hear:
When nibbling Sheep at large pursue their Food,
And unmolested Kine rechew the Cud;
When Curlews cry beneath the Village-walls, 35
And to her straggling Brood the Partridge calls;
Their short-liv'd Jubilee the Creatures keep,
Which but endures, whilst Tyrant-Man do's sleep;
When a sedate Content the Spirit feels,
And no fierce Light disturbs, whilst it reveals; 40
But silent Musings urge the Mind to seek
Something, too high for Syllables to speak;
Till the free Soul to a compos'dness charm'd,
Finding the Elements of Rage disarm'd,
O'er all below a solemn Quiet grown, 45
Joys in th' inferiour World, and thinks it like her Own:
In such a Night let me abroad remain,
Till Morning breaks, and All's confus'd again;
Our Cares, our Toils, our Clamours are renew'd,

50   Or Pleasures, seldom reach'd, again pursu'd.

　　　あのような夜，ひときわ騒々しい風がみな
　　　その遠くの洞窟に無事閉じ込められて，
　　　優しい西風だけがそよそよとその翼を震わせ，
　　　もの悲しい夜啼鳥がいつも目を覚まして歌う頃，
5 　　あるいは何処かの樹から，ふくろうが喜ぶ樹と名高いが，
　　　澄んだ声で呼びかけて，さすらう人に道を正しく教える頃.
　　　あのような夜，通りがかりの雲が次々と続き，
　　　あるいは空の神秘な顔に薄いヴェイルをかける頃.
　　　緑に覆われた，どこかの川に
10 　ゆらゆら揺れる月影と震える木の葉が見える頃.
　　　甦った草が今や身をすっくともたげ，
　　　涼しい土手を楽しい憩いへと招き，
　　　そこからスイカズラやイヌバラが芽を出し，
　　　眠たげな九輪桜が頭を隠して育つところ.
15 　一方ジギタリスは今やひときは淡い色を帯び，
　　　それでも浅黒い茂みにいつも赤い染みをつける頃.
　　　あちこち散らばる蛍らは，夕闇でこそ見事ゆえ，
　　　不美人に引き立つ時機を教えるが，
　　　友のソールズベリはどんな光にも合格で，
20 　完璧な魅力と完璧な美徳に輝いて.
　　　芳しい香りは，厭わしい昼を斥けていたが，
　　　穏やかな夜気の中を絶え間なく漂う.
　　　黒ずんだ木立ちがこの上なく柔らかな影を帯びて
　　　流れ落ちる水の音がはっきりと聞こえる頃.

薄暗がりのなか一層神さびて見えるのは 25
どこかの古い建物, 閑寂の中にも畏敬の念を起こさせる.
他方, 日焼けした丘がその茶褐色の貌を隠し,
かさばる乾草の山が谷間の影を濃く太くする.
放牧の馬が今や, 牧草の導くがままに,
近くの牧場の中をゆっくりと草を食みながらやって来る. 30
その忍び寄る足音と, 長く伸びた影に私たちはおびえ,
遂にはまぐさの噛み裂かれる音がする.
放たれて草をかじる羊らは己の食物を追い求め,
雌牛らは悠々と餌を戻しては反芻をする.
その頃シギは村の壁の下で鳴き, 35
ヤマウズラははぐれた雛たちに呼びかける.
生き物たちははかなくも喜びの時を祝うのだ,
暴君たる人間が眠る間だけしか続かぬが.
その頃, 霊魂はもの静かな満足を覚え,
それが秘密を明かす間は, どんな激しい光もかき乱すこ
となく, 40
静かな想いが心を駆り立てる
何か, 言葉に尽くせぬ高きものへ.
遂には自由な魂が魅せられて落ち着き,
凶暴な自然の力もいつしか和らげられて,
天が下の万物を厳かな静寂が支配し, 45
下界の自然にも喜びを見出し, 己に似た世界と観ずる.
そのような夜, わたしは戸外に留まっていたい.
やがて夜が明け, すべてが再び雑然と化し,
人の世のしがらみ, 労苦, 喧騒が新たに始まる,

50 　　あるいは快楽を,滅多に手には届かぬが,
　　　また追い求めゆく.

　このように,この詩「夜の夢想」は,『ベニスの商人』第5幕の冒頭シーン,あの甘美な夜の描写を始める 'In such a Night' のリフレインを借りながら,初めは風,鳥,雲,草花,馬や羊などの細かく具象的な自然描写から,次第に感情が高揚し,遂には夜の静寂と瞑想の中で霊的な歓喜を謳うところ,いかにもワーズワース好み,結びは夜の果てに訪れる昼の人間世界の苦しみを暗示して,ロマン的な哀感を漂わせた夜の賛歌となっている.

　　2　George, Lord Lyttelton, 'To the Memory of a Lady: A Monody'

　次は,イギリスの政治家・詩人で Sir Robert Walpole の政敵,Pope や Fielding と親しく,Thomson のパトロンでもあった初代男爵リットルトン卿(1709-73)の長詩「ある夫人の霊に捧げる哀歌」(1747)[3] を紹介しよう.

　英詩の挽歌としては,Milton の *Lycidas* (1638), Shelley の *Adonais* (1821), Tennyson の *In Memoriam* (1850), Arnold の *Thyrsis* (1866) などが名高いが,いずれも男性の友人を悼む類型的なコンベンションに則って,哲学的な死生観の披瀝を中心とするものが多い.

　これに対し,リットルトン卿の妻の死を悼む挽歌の場合はどうであろうか.一節ずつ試訳してみよう.

V　ロマン詩

To the Memory of a Lady
A Monody

　　In vain I look around
　　　O'er the well-known ground,
My Lucy's wonted footsteps to descry;
　　　Where oft we us'd to walk,
　　　Where oft in tender talk
We saw the summer sun go down the sky;
　　　Nor by yon fountain's side,
　　　Nor where its waters glide
Along the valley, can she now be found:
In all the wide-stretch'd prospect's ample bound
　　　No more my mournful eye
　　　Can aught of her espy,
But the sad sacred earth where her dear relics lie.

空^{むな}しくも私はあたりを見回す
よく見慣れた土地を,
わがルーシーのいつもの足取りを見つけようとして.
しばしば共に歩いたところ,
しばしば優しい会話を交わしながら
夏の太陽が沈むのを眺めたところだ.
また向こうの泉の傍でも
またその水が滑り流れて
谷に沿うところでも, 彼女はもう見つからぬ.

遠くまで眺望のきく広大な区域の中でも
もはや私の悲しみに沈む眼は
彼女の片鱗も認めることができない,
ただ彼女のいとしい遺骸の横たわる悲しくも
聖なる土(つち)を除いては.

O shades of Hagley, where is now your boast?
　　Your bright inhabitant is lost,
You she preferr'd to all the gay resorts
Where female vanity might wish to shine,
The pomp of cities, and the pride of courts.
Her modest beauties shunn'd the public eye:
　　To your sequestred dales
　　And flow'r-embroider'd vales
From an admiring world she chose to fly;
With Nature there retir'd, and Nature's God,
　　The silent paths of wisdom trod,
And banish'd ev'ry passion from her breast,
　　But those, the gentlest, and the best,
Whose holy flames with energy divine
The virtuous heart enliven and improve,
The conjugal, and the maternal love.

おお, ハグレー屋敷の木蔭よ, お前の誇りは今どこにある?
お前の立派な住人は亡くなったのだ.

V ロマン詩

お前を彼女はどんな賑やかな行楽地よりも好んだものだ．
女の虚栄心でとかく人目につきたい場所なのに，
都会の虚飾，宮廷の驕慢．
彼女の慎ましい美しさは人目を避けて，
お前の人里離れた谷間へと
人の賞めそやす世界から彼女は急ぎ立ち去ることに決めたのだ．
自然と共に．引き籠もり，自然の神とも共に．
知恵の静かな小道を踏みしめて，
胸からは激情をすべて払い除けたのだ．
ただ，あのこの上なく優しい，最善の情，
その聖なる焔が神々しい力をもって
高潔な心を活気づけ，向上させる
夫婦の，そして母性的な愛情のほかは．

Sweet babes, who, like the little playful fawns,
Were wont to trip along these verdant lawns
　　By your delighted mother's side,
　　Who now your infant steps shall guide?
Ah! where is now the hand whose tender care
To ev'ry virtue would have form'd your youth,
And strew'd with flow'rs the thorny ways of truth?
　　　O loss beyond repair!
　　O wretched father! left alone
To weep their dire misfortune, and thy own!
How shall thy weaken'd mind, oppress'd with woe,

  And drooping o'er thy Lucy's grave,
 Perform the duties that you doubly owe,
   Now she, alas! is gone,
From folly, and from vice, their helpless age to save?

   . . . .

可愛い赤子たちは，遊び好きの仔鹿のように，
この緑の芝生の上を軽やかに跳んでいたものだ，
お前たちの嬉しそうな母親の傍で．
誰が今お前たちの幼い歩みを導くのだろうか？
ああ！今やあの手はどこに，優しい心遣いで，
あらゆる美徳へと若いお前たちを育てたり，
真実の茨の道を花で飾ってくれただろうに．
おお取り返しのつかぬ損失！
おお哀れな父! 独り残されて
嘆く，赤子らの恐ろしい不幸，そして自分自身の不運!
どうすれば，おまえの気弱になった心が，悲しみに打ちひしがれて，
お前のルーシーの墓にうなだれて，
お前が二重に背負う務めを果たしていかれよう，
ああ悲し，彼女が逝った今，
愚かさから，悪徳から，赤子らの寄る辺ない歳月を守ってやるために？

O best of wives! O dearer far to me
 Than when thy virgin charms
 Were yielded to my arms,

How can my soul endure the loss of thee?
How in the world, to me a desert grown,
 Abandon'd, and alone,
Without my sweet companion can I live?
 Without thy lovely smile,
The dear reward of ev'ry virtuous toil,
What pleasures now can pall'd ambition give?
Ev'n the delightful sense of well-earn'd praise,
Unshar'd by thee, no more my lifeless thoughts could raise.

おお限りなく良き妻よ！ おお私には更にいとしい
君の純潔の魅力が
私の両腕にゆだねられた時よりも．
どうすれば，私の魂は君を失ったことに耐えられようか？
どうすれば，砂漠と化したこの世に，
見捨てられ，独りにされて，
優しい伴侶がなくて生きていかれよう？
君の愛らしい微笑みは
実直な骨折りの貴重な報酬，それなしに
大望もいま棺衣に包まれて，どんな楽しみを作り出せようというのか？
見事に勝ち得た賞賛の快感すらも，
君と分かち合えず，はや私の生気なき想いを高めようがないのだ．

 For my distracted mind

What succour can I find?
On whom for consolation shall I call?
　Support me, ev'ry friend,
　　Your kind assistance lend
To bear the weight of this oppressive woe.
　Alas! each friend of mine,
My dear, departed love, so much was thine,
That none has any comfort to bestow.
　My books, the best relief
　　In ev'ry other grief,
Are now with your idea sadden'd all:
Each fav'rite author we together read
My tortur'd mem'ry wounds, and speaks of Lucy dead.

私の取り乱した心に
どんな助けが見付けられようか?
誰に慰めを求めればよいのか?
私を支えてくれ,すべての友よ,
君等の優しい力を添えてくれ
この重苦しい悲痛の重荷に堪えるため.
ああ悲し! 私の友ひとりひとりが,
いとしい亡き人よ,まったく君のものだったから,
誰ひとり与える慰めを持ち合わせないのだ.
私の本は,最善の気晴らし
あらゆる他の嘆きの中でなら.
だが今は君の想いで悲しみに沈ませる,

V ロマン詩　　　　　　　　　75

一緒に読んだ好みの作家ひとりひとりが
私の追想を責め苛み，ルーシーの死を物語る．

We were the happiest pair of human kind!
The rolling year its varying course perform'd,
　　And back return'd again;
Another, and another smiling came,
And saw our happiness unchang'd remain:
　　Still in her golden chain
Harmonious Concord did our wishes bind:
　　Our studies, pleasures, tastes, the same.
　　　　O fatal, fatal stroke,
That all this pleasing fabric Love had rais'd
　　　　Of rare felicity,
On which ev'n wanton Vice with envy gaz'd,
And every scheme of bliss our hearts had form'd
With soothing hope, for many a future day,
　　In one sad moment broke!
Yet, O my soul, thy rising murmurs stay,
Nor dare th' all-wise Disposer to arraign,
　　Or against his supreme decree
　　With impious grief complain.
　That all thy full-blown joys at once should fade,
Was his most righteous will, and be that will obey'd.
　　　　　　　　　　　　　　Monody, 1747

私等は幸福至極な夫婦であった！
　　めぐる歳月はその移ろう歩みを果たし，
　　そして再び戻ってくれた．
　　また一年，また一年が微笑みながら訪れて，
　　私等の幸福が変わりなく続くのを見届けた．
　　いつも彼女の黄金の鎖の中で
　　私等の願いは琴瑟和して結ばれた，
　　私等の勉強，楽しみ，趣味を同じくし．
　　おお無惨な，無惨な一撃，
　　愛が建てていたこの心地好い建物は
　　稀に見る至福に満ちていて，
　　いたずらな悪徳すらも妬ましく見詰めたものだ．
　　私等の心が作り上げていた幸せの計画すべて，
　　心やわらぐ希望をもって，将来の日々に備えていたが，
　　それが悲しい一瞬のうちに破れたのだ！
　　だが，おお私の魂よ，お前の募るつぶやきは止めよ，
　　また全知の支配者を糾弾するな，
　　あるいはその至上の神意に逆らって
　　不遜な嘆きに溺れるな．
　　お前の咲き揃う喜びもみな直ぐに色褪せる，
　　それが公正極まる神の御心，それならばその御心に従う
　　ばかり．

　このように，妻の死を悼んだこの挽歌は，家政を申し分なく取りしきった主婦として，幼な子らを教え育てた母として，魂の伴侶としての妻を偲び，琴瑟相和した夫婦の人間的幸福を想

V ロマン詩

いつつ，もはや慰める術もない人生ながら，遂にはそれも神の摂理と悟り，敬虔な諦念へと向かう心境を述べた痛切な追悼歌となっている．

　しかし，実はここに収録された哀歌は全19連中の6連に過ぎない．つまり『オックスフォード18世紀詩集』の編者が，前半の第4，第5，第6の3連と後半の第16，第17，第18の3連を選んで巧みに結び合わせていたのである．[4]

　この省略部分を検討してみると，寂しい隠栖の場で悲しみのすべてを吐露しようと歌い出す冒頭3連はともかく，省略された第7連から第15連にかけて，例えば第8連だけでも，冷酷な運命から愛する妻を守れなかった詩神ミューズたちの無力を嘆きながら，ギリシアのPindus山脈や神泉のあるCastaliaの野，Aganippeの泉，悲劇詩人Thespisの谷，ヴァージルの生地を流れるMincio川，ローマ詩人Propertiusの住んだUmbria地方のClitumnus川，ホラティウスの別荘地Tivoliを流れるAnio川，ホメロスの生地IoniaのMeles川，そしてアテネのIlissus川を次々と羅列的に歌い込むところ，また第10連では自らを不幸なPetrarchに，妻をより美しいLauraに擬して，一掬の涙を流し，哀愁に満ちた歌を捧げよとミューズに会い，さらに第11連から第12連では'Vice', 'Truth', 'Virtue', 'Fortune', 'Interest', 'Ambition', 'Wisdom', 'Benevolence', 'Modesty', 'Suspicion'と大文字つきの抽象名詞を交えて妻ルーシーの人柄を讃え，その人生の盛事に死に襲われたことを嘆き，そして第13連，いかにも華麗な比喩をちりばめた1連が次のように続くのである．

So, where the silent streams of Liris glide,
In the soft bosom of Campania's vale,
When now the wintry tempests all are fled,
And genial Summer breathes her gentle gale,
The verdant orange lifts its beauteous head:
From every branch the balmy flowerets rise,
On every bough the golden fruits are seen;
With odours sweet it fills the smiling skies,
The wood-nymphs tend, and th' Idalian queen.
But, in the midst of all its blooming pride,
A sudden blast from Apenninus blows,
   Cold with perpetual snows:
The tender blighted plant shrinks up its leaves, and dies.

そうなのだ，リリスの静かな川が音もなく流れるところ,
カンパニアの谷の柔らかい胸に包まれて,
時はいま冬の嵐がみな飛び去って,
快い夏がその優しい風を息吹く頃.
新緑のオレンジがその美しい頭をもたげ
どの枝からも香りのよい小さな花が咲き,
どの大枝にも黄金の果実が見えて,
甘い匂いで微笑む空を一杯にする,
森の精が，そしてイダリアの女王が，それを見守る.
だがしかし，その咲き誇るさなかに,
アペニンの山から一陣の風が吹き来たり,
   万年雪で冷えきった風に,

いたいけな草花は打ち枯らされて，
その葉を縮め，死に絶える．

　このように，温暖なオレンジの薫る風土とそれを襲うアペニン山脈から吹き荒ぶ寒風との対比によって，幸福な夫婦愛が一挙に引き裂かれたことを比喩したのである．

　こうして省略された幾つかの連を読み併せてくると，Sutherland 教授が前述の講義録で指摘したように，[5] この「哀歌」全篇には明らかに二つの声がある．つまり，リットルトン卿の心情表白の詩行と必ずしも不誠実とはいえぬ詩的装飾に満ちた詩行とが共存していたのである．しかも後者の声の量が大きい．これはワーズワースの『抒情民謡詩集』の「序文」(1800)のいわゆる「力強い感情がおのずから流露したもの」('the spontaneous overflow of powerful feelings') だけに留まらない．そこには真率な悲歎をのべる部分とそれを抑制する部分の二重構造があって，この「哀歌」もやはり他の伝統的な挽歌の例に洩れず，一種の 18 世紀風挽歌の変奏曲ということになろうか．

注

1) Wordsworth, 'Essay, Supplement to the Preface' in *The Poetical Works of Wordsworth*, ed. Thomas Hutchinson (1904; rev. Ernest de Selincourt, Oxford Univ. Press, 1960), p.747.

2) *Early Eighteenth Century Poetry*, ed. James Sutherland (Edward Arnold, 1965), pp. 33-4.

3) *18th V*, No.211, pp.309-12.
4) 'To the Memory of the Same Lady. A Monody. A. D. 1747' in *The Works of the English Poets, from Chaucer to Cowper,* ed. by Alexander Chalmers, Vol.XIV (1810; rpt. Hildesheim・New York: Georg Olms Verlag, 1970), pp.180-2.
5) James Sutherland, *A Preface to Eighteenth Century Poetry* (1948; rpt. Oxford University Press Paperbacks, 1963), pp.71-4.

VI 物語詩

1 Frances Seymour, Countess of Hertford, 'The Story of Inkle and Yarico'

二つの物語詩を紹介しよう．一つは先きのウィンチルシー伯爵夫人が大伯母に当たる才女ハートフォード伯爵夫人（1699–1754）の「インクルとヤリコの物語」（1726?）[1] である．これは Steele が *The Spectator* (No.11, 13 March 1711) で発表した翻案の話を，彼女が次のように heroic couplet で 104 行の韻文に仕立てたものである．

The Story of Inkle and Yarico.
A most moving Tale from the Spectator [*No.11*]

A YOUTH there was possessed of every charm,
Which might the coldest heart with passion warm;
His blooming cheeks with ruddy beauty glowed,
His hair in waving ringlets graceful flowed;
Through all his person an attractive mien,
Just symmetry, and elegance were seen:
But niggard Fortune had her aid withheld,

    And poverty th' unhappy boy compelled
    To distant climes to sail in search of gain,
10 Which might in ease his latter days maintain.
    By chance, or rather the decree of Heaven,
    The vessel on a barbarous coast was driven;
    He, with a few unhappy striplings more,
    Ventured too far upon the fatal shore:
    The cruel natives thirsted for their blood,
    And issued furious from a neighbouring wood.
    His friends all fell by brutal rage o'erpowered,
    Their flesh the horrid cannibals devoured;
    Whilst he alone escaped by speedy flight,
20 And in a thicket lay concealed from sight!

あらゆる魅力を備えた若者がいた,
どんなに冷たい心でも情熱で熱くするほどの.
若さに輝く頬は血色よい美しさで紅潮し,
髪は波打つ巻毛となって優美に垂れた.
全身に人目を引きつける様子,
見事な均整と優雅さが見られた.
だが, けちな運命の女神は手助けを惜しみ,
不運な少年は貧しさに駆り立てられて,
一旗揚げんと遠国へ船出した,
10 後の日々を安楽に暮らせもしようと.
だが偶然に. いやむしろ天の定めによって,
船はとある未開の海辺に押し流された.

VI　物語詩　　　　　　　　　　　83

彼は不運な若者数人とともに
宿命の陸地に踏み込みすぎた．
残忍な土人たちが彼等の血を求めて渇き，
近くの林から荒れ狂って躍り出た．
友はみな野蛮な憤怒に打ち倒されて，
彼等の肉を忌まわしい食人鬼どもがくらった．
彼ひとり素早く逃げて脱出し，
茂みに隠れ人目につかず横たわったのだ！　　　　　　　　20

　Now he reflects on his companions' fate,
His threatening danger, and abandoned state.
Whilst thus in fruitless grief he spent the day,
A negro virgin chanced to pass that way;
He viewed her naked beauties with surprise,
Her well-proportioned limbs and sprightly eyes!
With his complexion and gay dress amazed,
The artless nymph upon the stranger gazed;
Charmed with his features and alluring grace,
His flowing locks and his enlivened face.　　　　　　　　30
His safety now became her tend'rest care,
A vaulted rock she knew and hid him there;
The choicest fruits the isle produced she sought,
And kindly to allay his hunger brought;
And when his thirst required, in search of drink,
She led him to a chrystal fountain's brink.
　Mutually charmed, by various arts they strove

To inform each other of their mutual love;
A language soon they formed, which might express
Their pleasing care and growing tenderness.
With tigers' speckled skins she decked his bed,
O'er which the gayest plumes of birds were spread;
And every morning, with the nicest care,
Adorned her well-turned neck and shining hair,
With all the glittering shells and painted flowers
That serve to deck the Indian virgins' bowers.
And when the sun descended in the sky,
And lengthening shades foretold the evening nigh,
Beneath some spreading palm's delightful shade,
Together sat the youth and lovely maid;
Or where some bubbling river gently crept,
She in her arms secured him while he slept.
When the bright moon in midnight pomp was seen,
And starlight glittered o'er the dewy green,
In some close arbour, or some fragrant grove,
He whispered vows of everlasting love.
Then, as upon the verdant turf he lay,
He oft would to th' attentive virgin say:
'Oh, could I but, my Yarico, with thee
Once more my dear, my native country see!
In softest silks thy limbs should be arrayed,
Like that of which the clothes I wear are made;
What different ways my grateful soul would find

VI 物語詩　　　　　　　　　85

To indulge thy person and divert thy mind!';
While she on the enticing accents hung
That smoothly fell from his persuasive tongue.

　さて今や若者は思案した，仲間たちの運命や
身に迫る危険やら，見捨てられた身の上を．
このように詮ない悲しみの日を送るうち，
黒人娘があたりを偶然通り過ぎ，
若者は娘の裸の美しさに驚いた，
均整のとれた手足と生き生きとした眼!
彼の顔色や華やかな服にあっけにとられ，
純真な娘はその見知らぬ人をじっと視た，
その目鼻立ち，魅惑的な優美さ，
ふさふさと垂れる髪，活気ある顔にうっとりとして．　　30
彼の安全が今一番の心配の種，
かねて知る丸天井のある岩に彼を隠し，
島きっての甘い果物を探し，
親切に運んでは彼の飢えをしずめた．
喉の渇きで，飲み物を求められると，
透き通る泉のほとりへ若者を導いた．
　互いに心惹かれ，二人はさまざまに手を尽くし
互いに愛を伝えんとした．
言葉を直ぐに二人は作り，それで表わす快い心遣いと募
る優しさ．　　　　　　　　　　　　　　　　　　40
虎の縞皮で彼女は彼の床を飾り，
その上に鳥の一番あでやかな羽毛を敷いた．

朝ごとに，この上なく念入りに
優美な襟首と輝く髪をととのえ，
きらめく貝殻と色とりどりの花で
インディアン娘らは寝室を飾るのだ．
そして太陽が西の空に沈み，
長びく影が近づく夕べを告げたとき，
枝を広げた棕櫚の楽しい木蔭に，
50 若者と可愛い乙女がともに座った．
あるいはどこかざわめく川が緩やかに流れるところで，
彼女は眠る若者を両腕に抱いた．
明るい月が夜半皓々と照らし，
星の光が露の降りた草地にきらめくと，
どこか秘密の木蔭か，どこか香り高い木立ちの中で，
彼は変わらぬ愛の誓いを囁いた．
それから緑の芝生に横になると，
よく彼は耳を傾ける娘にこう言ったものだ．
「ああ，もし僕が，僕のヤリコよ，お前と一緒に
60 もう一度，僕の懐かしい，生まれ故郷を見られたらなあ！
一番柔らかい絹でお前の手足を飾ってあげよう，
いま僕が着ている絹地のような．
僕の感謝に満ちた魂がいろんな遣り方を見つけて
お前の体をくつろがせ，心を喜ばせたいのだ！
その間，彼女は心をそそる言葉にじっと聴き入った．
彼の説得力ある口からすらすらと出て来たものだから．

　　One evening, from a rock's impending side,

An European vessel she descried,
And made them signs to touch upon the shore,
Then to her lover the glad tidings bore;   70
Who with his mistress to the ship descends,
And found the crew were countrymen and friends.
Reflecting now upon the time he passed,
Deep melancholy all his thoughts o'ercast:
'Was it for this,' said he, 'I crossed the main,
Only a doting virgin's heart to gain ?
I needed not for such a prize to roam,
There are a thousand doting maids at home.'
While thus his disappointed mind was tossed,
The ship arrived on the Barbadian coast;   80
Immediately the planters from the town,
Who trade for goods and negro slaves, came down;
And now his mind, by sordid interest swayed,
Resolved to sell his faithful Indian maid.
Soon at his feet for mercy she implored,
And thus in moving strains her fate deplored:

 'O whither can I turn to seek redress,
When thou'rt the cruel cause of my distress?
If the remembrance of our former love,
And all thy plighted vows, want force to move;   90
Yet, for the helpless infant's sake I bear,
Listen with pity to my just despair.
Oh let me not in slavery remain,

Doomed all my life to drag a servile chain!
It cannot surely be! thy generous breast
An act so vile, so sordid must detest:
But, if thou hate me, rather let me meet
A gentler fate, and stab me at thy feet;
Then will I bless thee with my dying breath,
100　And sink contented in the shades of death.'
　　Not all she said could his compassion move,
Forgetful of his vows and promised love;
The weeping damsel from his knees he spurned,
And with her price pleased to the ship returned.

(1726?)

　ある夕べ,岩の張り出た端から
ヨーロッパの船を彼女が発見し
岸辺に寄るよう合図を送る,
70　恋する人に嬉しい知らせ.
彼は恋人とその船へと乗り込んだ,
船員は同胞の味方だと知れたのだ.
さて今や彼は来し方を想いつつ,
深い憂鬱に心をすっかり閉ざされた.
「こんなことのためだったのか」と彼は言う,「僕が海を渡ったのは,
ただ他愛ない娘の心を得んがため?
こんな褒美を欲しがって,さまよう必要はなかったのだ,
恋に溺れる娘なら故郷にごまんといるだろう」

このように落胆で彼の心は揺れたまま，
船はバルバドスの岸辺に着いた． 80
すぐに町から植民者たちが
品物や黒人奴隷の商売にやって来た．
今や彼は卑しい欲に目がくらみ，
忠実なインディアン娘を売る決心．
彼の足元に伏して彼女は慈悲を乞い，
このように涙声にて悲運を嘆く．
「どこを向いて救いを求めたらよいのでしょう？
わたしの苦しみは酷いあなたのせいだもの．
これまでの愛の思い出と
誓いの約束すべてでも，あなたの心が動かないなら， 90
せめて身籠もった寄る辺ない赤子のために，
当然の絶望を哀れと聴いて．
ああ，どうか奴隷のままに捨てないで，
死ぬまで奴隷の鎖を引きずらせるなんて！
そんなことがあるかしら！ あなたは心の広い方，
そんな卑劣な，浅ましい所業はとてもできぬ筈．
でも，もしもわたしがとても憎いなら，いっそ会わせて
欲しいもの，
もっと優しい運命に，ひと突きあなたの足許で．
それなら息も絶え絶えにあなたのことを祝福し，
思い残すことなく死の陰の谷に沈みましょう」 100
　これだけ言われても，彼は憐れみはしなかった．
誓いと約束の愛を忘れ果て．
涙ながらの乙女を縋る膝から足蹴にし，

彼女の売値に喜んで彼は船へと帰って行った.

　このように, 西インド諸島 Barbados 付近を背景にして, 不実な白人青年と純愛を捧げたインディアン娘の悲恋に終わる話は, 当時流行の題材らしく, George Colman the Younger (1762-1836) の劇 *Inkle and Yarico* (1787) によっても取り上げられている. 18世紀イギリスで夥しい「架空航海記」が出版されているように,[2] 西欧が世界に進出した大航海時代の夢まだ醒めやらず, 人々の間に海外への好奇心と異国情緒を楽しむ雰囲気が色濃く残っていたのであろう. そして同時に, この異国趣味愛好とともに, 未開の地で文明に毒されぬ島娘 Yarico のなかに「高貴な野蛮人」('the noble savage') に象徴される原始崇拝への憧れが秘められているのではなかろうか. さらに今日的な解釈を加えるとすれば, このような話は原住民側にとって単なる悲恋物語ではすまされまい. 差別と搾取を事とする人種問題をからめた植民地主義批判, いわゆる Post-colonial 批評に通じるものがあるかもしれない.

　それにしても, 異国趣味の物語詩と heroic couplet 詩形の取り合わせは, いささか奇異な感じがしないでもない. いや, それほどまでに2行連句が詩作の金科玉条として18世紀を風靡していたということか, 次のバラッド調物語詩についても同様のことが言えるであろう.

2　Lady Anne Lindsay, (*later* Barnard) 'Auld Robin Gray'

　もう一つの物語詩は, 当時絶大な人気を博したバラッド風,

VI 物語詩　　　　　　　　　91

後の Tennyson の有名な詩 *Enoch Arden*（1864）と同工異曲，スコットランド出身のこれまた才女リンジー女史（1750－1825）の21才頃の作「老ロビン・グレイ」（1771）[3] である．早速，試訳に移ろう．

Auld Robin Gray

W<small>HEN</small> the sheep are in the fauld, when the cows come hame,
When a' the weary world to quiet rest are gane,
The woes of my heart fa' in showers frae my ee,
Unken'd by my gudeman, who soundly sleeps by me.

羊が檻に，雌牛は小屋に．
人みな疲れ静かに休む頃，
哀しみがあたしの目からどっと落ち，
夫は知らぬ，あたしの傍で眠りこけ．

Young Jamie loo'd me weel, and sought me for his bride;
But saving ae crown-piece, he'd naething else beside.
To make the crown a pound, my Jamie gaed to sea;
And the crown and the pound, oh! they were baith for me!

若いジェイミが愛してくれて，あたしをお嫁に欲しがっ

た,
1文銀があるだけで, あの人ほかに何もなく,
1文を大金にしようとて, ジェイミは海に乗り出した.
大枚小枚, ああ, みんなあたしのためだった!

Before he had been gane a twelvemonth and a day,
10　My father brak his arm, our cow was stown away;
My mither she fell sick — my Jamie was at sea —
And auld Robin Gray, oh! he came a-courting me.

1年と1日経たぬ間に,
10　父さん腕折り, 雌牛が盗まれ,
母さん発病－ジェイミは海で－
そうして老いたロビン・グレイ, ああ! あの人あたしに
言い寄った.

My father cou'dna work, my mother cou'dna spin;
I toil'd day and night, but their bread I cou'dna win;
And Rob maintain'd them baith, and, wi' tears in his ee,
Said, 'Jenny, oh! for their sakes, will you marry me?'

あたしの父さん働けず, 母さん糸も紡げずで,
あたしが夜昼あくせくと, それでも暮らしが立てられず,
ロブが二親看てくれて, 目には涙でいうことにゃ,
「ジェニー, なあ! 親のため, おいらと結婚する気はな

いか？」

My heart it said na, and I look'd for Jamie back;
But hard blew the winds, and his ship was a wrack:
His ship it was a wrack! Why didna Jenny dee?
Or, wherefore am I spared to cry out, Woe is me! 20

その気になれず断って，ジェイミの帰りを待ちわびた．
けれども風が吹き荒れて，ジェイミの船は難破した．
ジェイミの船が難破した！ ジェニーはどうして死ななんだ？
どうして泣かずにおられよう，ああ悲し！ 20

My father argued sair—my mother didna speak,
But she look'd in my face till my heart was like to break:
They gied him my hand, but my heart was in the sea;
And so auld Robin Gray, he was gudeman to me.

父さん本気で説き伏せた－母さんは口きかず，
あたしの顔を覗き込み，あたしの心は破れそう，
親が結婚承知した，それでも心は外の海．
こうして老いたロビンが，あたしの夫．

I hadna been his wife, a week but only four,
When mournfu' as I sat on the stane at my door,

I saw my Jamie's ghaist—I cou'dna think it he,
Till he said, 'I'm come hame, my love, to marry thee!'

女房になって4週もまだ立たぬうち,
悲しくて戸口の石に座っていると,
ジェイミの幽霊が目に見えた－人違いかと思ったが,
とうとう幽霊こう言った,「帰って来たよ, いとしいお前, お前と結婚するために!」

O sair, sair did we greet, and mickle say of a';
30   Ae kiss we took, nae mair—I bad him gang awa.
I wish that I were dead, but I'm no like to dee;
For O, I am but young to cry out, Woe is me!

おお, わたしらは涙, 涙の物語, 話はみんなしたけれど,
30   一度の口付け, それだけで－遠くへ行ってと言いつけた.
死んでいればと思いつつ, だけれどそうもなりません.
だって, あたしは若いもの, ああ悲しいと叫ぶだけ!

I gang like a ghaist, and I carena much to spin;
I darena think o' Jamie, for that wad be a sin.
But I will do my best a gude wife aye to be,
For auld Robin Gray, oh! he is sae kind to me.
(Wr. 1771; pub. 1776)

あたしはまるで幽霊みたい, 紡ぎ仕事も身が入らぬ,

ジェイミのことは思うまい，だってそれでは罪になる．
精一杯いついつまでも良い妻に，
老いたロビンのために，ああ！あの人とっても優しいの．

注

1) *18th WP.* No.77, pp.106-9.
2) Cf. P.B.Gove, *The Imaginary Voyage in Prose Fiction. A History of its Criticism and a Guide for its Study, with an Annotated Check List of 215 Imaginary Voyages from 1700 to 1800* (1941; rpt. New York: Octagon Books, 1975).
3) *New 18th V,* No.369, pp.573-4. *The Literary Ballad,* ed. Anne Henry Ehrenpreis (Edward Arnold, 1966), pp.49-51.

VII 動物愛の詩

1 Robert Burns, 'To a Mouse'

スコットランドの国民詩人ロバート・バーンズ（1759-96）の詩「ハツカネズミへ, 鋤で巣を掘り起こした折に, 1785年11月」(1786)[1] から動物愛の詩を始めよう.

To a Mouse, On turning her up in her Nest, with the Plough, November, 1785

Wee, sleeket, cowran, tim'rous beastie,
O, what a panic's in thy breastie!
Thou need na start awa sae hasty,
    Wi' bickering brattle!
I wad be laith to rin an' chase thee,
    Wi' murd'ring pattle!

I'm truly sorry man's domimion
Has broken Nature's social union,
An' justifies that ill opinion,
    Which makes thee startle,

Ⅶ 動物愛の詩

At me, thy poor, earth-born companion,
　　　　　An' fellow-mortal!

I doubt na, whyles, but thou may thieve;
What then? poor beastie, thou maun live!
A daimen-icker in a thrave
　　　　　'S a sma' request:
I'll get a blessin wi' the lave,
　　　　　An' never miss 't!

ちっちゃな，つやつやした毛の，すくんで臆病な動物よ．
おお，お前の小さな胸のうち，なんとおびえていることか！
そんなに急いで逃げ出さなくてもいいんだよ．
　　　　　せかせか慌てふためいて！
走って追いかけたりはしやしない．
　　　　　命をあやめる鋤もって！

ほんとにご免，威張りくさった人間が
自然の楽しい交わりをぶち壊す，
悪い評判もっともだ，
　　　　　それでお前もぎょっとする，
わしを見て怖がって，同じ土から生まれた相棒で，
　　　　　土に帰る仲間なのに！

10

そりゃ時にはお前でも盗みをせんとは思わない．

それがどうした？　かわいそうな動物よ，お前だって生きなくちゃ！
刈り束の穂の一本ぐらい
　　　　　　そりゃ僅かな要求だ．
俺は残りのもので幸せで，
　　　　　　惜しくも何とも思わない！

Thy wee-bit housie, too, in ruin!
20　　It's silly wa's the win's are strewin!
An' naething, now, to big a new ane,
　　　　　　O' foggage green!
An' bleak December's winds ensuin,
　　　　　　Baith snell an' keen!

Thou saw the fields laid bare an' wast
An' weary winter comin fast,
An' cozie here, beneath the blast,
　　　　　　Thou thought to dwell,
Till crash! the cruel coulter past
30　　　　　　Out through thy cell.

That wee-bit heap o' leaves an' stibble,
Has cost thee monie a weary nibble!
Now thou's turned out, for a' thy trouble,
　　　　　　But house or hald,

To thole the winter's sleety dribble,
        An' cranreuch cauld!

お前のちっちゃなお家もこける!
もろい壁なんか風が吹いてまき散らす!
もう何もない,新しいお家を作るにも,
        緑の雑草,何もない!
寒い師走の風が続いて吹いて,
        身を刺すように骨にもしみる!

野っ原が裸になって荒れはてて,
つらい冬が駆け足で来ても,
お前はここで心地よく,突風なんかどこ吹く風と,
        住めば都ときめこんだ,
ところがガシャー! 情けを知らぬ鋤の刃が
        お前の庵を貫いた.

葉っぱと刈り株のあの小山,
お前にゃ苦労の家普請!
だのにお前は追い出され,骨折り損で
        隠れ場もない家のそと,
耐えなきゃならぬ冬みぞれ,
        それに身を切る寒い霜!

But mousie, thou art no thy-lane,
In proving foresight may be vain:

The best laid schemes o' mice an' men
    Gang aft agley,
An' lea'e us nought but grief an' pain,
    For promised joy!

Still, thou art blest, compared wi' me!
The present only toucheth thee:
But Och! I backward cast my e'e
    On prospects drear!
An' forward, though I canna see,
    I guess an' fear!

            (1786)

sleeket] glossy bickering brattle] scurrying haste pattle] spade whyles] at times daimen-icker] odd ear of corn thrave] two stooks lave] remainder big] build foggage] coarse grass snell] bitter But] without hald] refuge thole] endure cranreuch] frost no thy-lane] not alone Gang aft agley] go oft awry

だがネズミ，お前だけではないのだよ，
先が読めぬは世の常だ．
ハツカネズミや人間のどんなに上手な企ても
    しょっちゅうしくじってしまうもの，
残るは嘆きと苦しみばかり，
    ぬか喜びというわけさ！

Ⅶ 動物愛の詩

それでもお前はいいほうだ，この俺さまと比べれば！
お前の難儀は今だけだ．
だがあ～あ，昔のほうに目をやりゃ
　　　　わびしい眺め！
先きのほうに目をやりゃ，見えないけれど，
　　　　当て推量で怖いのだ！

　このように，ネズミも人間と同様，神によって土で作られ土に帰る生き物，バーンズにとっては他人事ではない．営々と築いた冬籠もり用の住み家が，青天の霹靂，一瞬のうちに破壊される．まさに人間は天敵に等しい．バーンズは小屋住みの農夫たる父親の教育を受けて育った．ネズミに寄せる愛情は貧しい農民に対する同情にも重なり，結局のところ弱者に君臨する暴君，上流特権階級の横暴そのものへの批判にも通じるのであろう．スコットランドの厳しい冬を背景にして，その方言を駆使したこの詩は，表面いかにも軽快ながら，正義感の強い民衆詩人バーンズの人間観や自然観を伝えて余す所がない．

2　John Dyer, 'My Ox Duke'
　もう一篇，ダイア（1699-1757）といえば主に地誌的な賛歌 *Grongar Hill*（1726）の作者として記憶されるが，ここではこのウェールズ生まれの詩人の動物愛と宗教心が融け合った詩「わが雄牛デューク」（1735?)[2] を取り上げておこう．

My Ox Duke

'Twas on a summer noon, in Stainsford mead
New mown and tedded, while the weary swains,
Louting beneath an oak, their toils relieved;
And some with wanton tale the nymphs beguiled,
And some with song, and some with kisses rude;
Their scythes hung o'er their heads: when my brown ox,
Old labourer Duke, in awkward haste I saw
Run stumbling through the field to reach the shade
Of an old open barn, whose gloomy floor
10   The lash of sounding flails had long forgot.
In vain his eager haste: sudden old Duke
Stopped; a soft of snow-white little pigs
Along the sacred threshold sleeping lay.
Burnt in the beam, and stung with swarming flies,
He stood tormented on the shadow's edge:
What should he do? What sweet forbearance held
His heavy foot from trampling on the weak,
To gain his wishes? Hither, hither all,
Ye vain, ye proud! see, humble heaven attends;
20   The fly-teased brute with gentle pity stays,
And shields the sleeping young. O gracious Lord!
Aid of the feeble, cheerer of distress,
In his low labyrinth each small reptile's guide!

Ⅶ　動物愛の詩　　　　　　　　　　　103

God of unnumbered worlds! Almighty power!
Assuage our pride. Be meek, thou child of man:
Who gives thee life, gives every worm to live,
Thy kindred of the dust.—Long waiting stood
The good old labourer, in the burning beam,
And breathed upon them, nosed them, touched them soft,
With lovely fear to hurt their tender sides; 30
Again soft touched them; gently moved his head
From one to one; again, with touches soft,
He breathed them o'er, till gruntling waked and stared
The merry little young, their tails upcurled,
And gambolled off with scattered flight. Then sprung
The honest ox, rejoiced, into the shade.

　　　　　　　　　　　(Wr. 1735?; pub. 1855)

　　　louting] lolling

とある夏の昼，スティンズフォードの牧場で
新しく刈った草が広げて干され，その間，疲れた田舎の若者たちが，
樫の木の下に寝そべって，仕事から解放されて一息，
ある者は浮気話で田舎娘たちを楽します，
またある者は歌で，ある者は荒っぽいキスで，
鎌は頭上に垂れかけたまま．その時わが褐色の雄牛どん，

働き手の老デューク，見るとぶざまな急ぎ足，
躓きながら野を走り日陰に入ろうと
古い開いた納屋めがけ，その薄暗い床板は
10 脱穀の鞭のひびきをとっくに忘れていたが．
老デューク本気で急いだ甲斐がない，突然に
ぱったり止まる．雪白の子豚らが柔らかい背を並べ
聖なる入口に沿って横になり眠ってた．
日射しに焼けて，群がるハエに刺されつつ，
雄牛は困りきり影の端に立ち往生．
どうしたらよいものか？ ほんとに優しく我慢して重い
足を止めたのだ，
弱いものらを踏みつけて，
自分の望みを遂げるより．ここでこそ，ここでみな，
汝ら自惚れ強き者，汝ら傲慢なる者! 見るがよい，つつ
ましき神が見そなわす．
20 ハエにじらされるあの牛は憐れに思いじっとして，
眠る子豚らをかばうのだ．おお慈悲深き主よ!
弱きを助け，悩める者を慰める方，
地中の迷路を這う小さなものを導くお方!
数知れぬ世界の神よ! 全能の力よ!
われらの高慢を鎮め給え．柔和なれ，汝 人の子よ，
汝に命を与える者が，すべての虫を生かすのだ，
汝と同じ塵の縁者を．——長らく立って待っていた．
その善良で老いた働き者は，焼けつく日射しの中で，
子豚らに息をかけ，鼻をすり寄せ，やさしく触れた．
30 柔らかい横腹を傷つけぬように気遣いながら．

再びやさしく触れた，そっと自分の頭を動かして
一匹から一匹へ．また，やさしく触れて，
息をかけると，子豚らはブーブー鳴いて目を覚まし目を
見張る
愉快なものたちだ，尻尾を捲き上げて，
慌てふためき，一目散に跳んで逃げた．そこでようやく
飛び込んだ
正直者の雄牛どん，いかにもうれしく，陰の中．

　このように，田舎の自然を背景に，老いた雄牛の子豚に寄せる優しさを謳いながら，神の生きとし生ける者への愛と人間の傲慢に対する戒めを説く教訓詩ともなっている．このような傾向は牧師となったダイアにふさわしいが，この動物詩についても，ジョンソン博士ならばその散文的な題材と冗長な歌いぶりを貶し，ワーズワースならばその清新素朴な自然描写を賞めることになるのであろうか．[3]

注

1) *New 18th V*, No.465, pp.706-7.

2) Ibid., No.125, p.171.

3) Cf.*The Oxford Companion to English Literature*, ed. Margaret Drabble (1985), p. 303.

VIII　フェミニズムの詩

1　Mary, Lady Chudleigh, 'To the Ladies'

いよいよ女流詩人たちに登場してもらおう．彼女たちの主要テーマはやはり女権拡張論であり，断るまでもないが，人間としての女性解放，具体的には選挙権，教育，結婚，家庭などにおける男女同権の主張にほかならない．

まず第一に，戦闘的な論客 Mary Astell (1666-1731) の影響を受けたチャドリ夫人 (1656-1710) の「淑女たちへ」('To the Ladies', 1703)[1] を取り上げてみよう．鮮明なフェミニズム宣言とでも称すべき2行連句の24行である．

To the Ladies

WIFE and servant are the same,
But only differ in the name:
For when that fatal knot is tied,
Which nothing, nothing can divide,
When she the word *Obey* has said,
And man by law supreme has made,
Then all that's kind is laid aside,

VIII フェミニズムの詩

And nothing left but state and pride.
Fierce as an eastern prince he grows,
And all his innate rigour shows:　　　　　　　　10
Then but to look, to laugh or speak,
Will the nuptial contract break.
Like mutes, she signs alone must make,
And never any freedom take,
But still be governed by a nod,
And fear her husband as her god:
Him still must serve, him still obey,
And nothing act, and nothing say,
But what her haughty lord thinks fit,
Who, with the power, has all the wit.　　　　　　20
Then shun, oh! shun that wretched state,
And all the fawning flatterers hate.
Value yourselves and men despise:
You must be proud, if you'll be wise.

(1703)

妻と召使いは同じこと，
違うのはただ名前だけ．
あの運命の絆が結ばれたら最後，
どうしても，どうしてもその結び目は断ち切れない．
妻が「従う」という言葉を言ってしまい，
夫を法によってこの上ない人にしてしまったら，
優しいことはみな捨て去られ，

身分と誇りのほかは何も残されぬ．
　　　夫は東方の君主のように威丈高になり，
10　　苛酷な本性を丸出しにする．
　　　そうなると，見たり，笑ったり，口をきくだけで，
　　　婚礼の誓いを破ることになる．
　　　啞のように，妻はただパントマイムをして，
　　　決して自由な振舞は許されず，
　　　いつも顎で使われて，
　　　夫を神と恐れる破目になる．
　　　いつも夫に仕え，いつも夫に従う掟，
　　　何もしない，何も言わない，
　　　横柄な主人がよしと認めることのほか，
20　　主人こそ，権力と，知恵のすべてを持つ人だ．
　　　だから遠ざかれ，ああ! 遠ざかれ，あの哀れな身分には，
　　　ご機嫌取りのおっぺか使いはみな憎め．
　　　自分が大事，男たちを見下して，
　　　賢くなるには誇りが必要．

　このように，彼女は17才で30才の男爵 Sir George Chudleigh と結婚し，孤独で知的刺激も乏しい不幸な生活を送った体験に基づいて，やがて女子教育の重要性を説くに至り，とりわけ夫への絶対服従を強いる結婚を戒めた．この詩は18世紀初頭の社会における女性の地位の低さを簡潔に物語っていよう．[2]

2 Mary Leapor, 'Upon her Play being returned to her, stained with Claret'

次に,結婚生活の幸不幸にかかわらず,もし仮に当時の女性がものを書き出版しようとしたらどうなるか,その一例をメアリ・リーポー (1722-46) の「脚本を手許に戻された折に,ぶどう酒の染みをつけられて」(1751)[3] にみよう.

Upon her Play being returned to her, stained with Claret

Welcome, dear wanderer, once more!
   Thrice welcome to thy native cell!
Within this peaceful humble door
   Let thou and I contented dwell!

But say, O whither hast thou ranged?
   Why dost thou blush a crimson hue?
Thy fair complexion's greatly changed:
   Why, I can scarce believe 'tis you.

Then tell, my son, O tell me, where
   Didst thou contract this sottish dye?
You kept ill company, I fear,
   When distant from your parent's eye.

Was it for this, O graceless child!

>   Was it for this you learned to spell?
>   Thy face and credit both are spoiled:
>   Go drown thyself in yonder well.
>
> I wonder how thy time was spent:
>   No news, alas, hast thou to bring?
> Hast thou not climbed the Monument?
>   Nor seen the lions, nor the King?
>
> But now I'll keep you here secure:
>   No more you view the smoky sky;
> The Court was never made, I'm sure,
>   For idiots like thee and I.

20

(Wr. by 1746; pub. 1751)

お帰り，いとしい放浪者よ，いま一度!
よくぞ帰った，お前の生まれた古巣へ!
この平和なあばら屋のなかで
お前とわたしは満足して暮らそう!

だが言っておくれ，おお，お前はどこをさ迷ってきたの?
なぜお前は深紅色に顔を赤らめるの?
お前の美しい顔色はすっかり変わって，
ほんと，昔のお前とはとても信じられない．

だから話しておくれ，わたしの息子よ，おお話しておく

VIII フェミニズムの詩

れ,どこで
お前はこんな飲んだくれの色に染まったの? 10
悪い仲間と付き合ったのか,とも案ずるが,
親の目から遠く離れて.

こんなことのためだったの,ああ堕落した子供よ!
こんなことのためだったの,お前がものを書くのを覚えたのは?
お前の顔も信用も台無しじゃない,
向こうの井戸に身を投げておしまい.

お前はどんな過ごし方をしたのかしらね.
どんな土産話も,まあ悲しい,お前は持って帰らないの?
お前は大火記念柱にも昇らなかったの?
ライオンも,また王様も見ずじまいなの? 20

でも今からはお前をここで守ってあげる,
煙たい空も見させはしない,
宮廷はもともと似合いじゃなかったのよ,きっと,
お前やわたしのような阿呆連れには.

　さて,彼女はさる貴族の屋敷の庭師の娘,正式の教育を受けることなく,幼少より読み書きを覚え,母親の制止を聴かず,母の死後は家政や女中奉公をしながら Dryden や Pope を真似て詩作したという.このパラッド調の軽快な詩には,一見,機知に溢れて遊戯的なところがあるが,案外,一抹の自嘲と淡い

抗議が込められているのかもしれない．とすれば，当然この早逝した薄幸の才女が次のような「女性論」('An Essay on Woman', 1751)⁴⁾ を書いたとしても頷けないことではない．その先鋭なフェミニズム主張の一節を紹介しておこう．

An Essay on Woman

  WOMAN, a pleasing but a short-lived flow'r,
 Too soft for business and weak for pow'r:
 A wife in bondage, or neglected maid;
 Despised, if ugly; if she's fair, betrayed.
 'Tis wealth alone inspires ev'ry grace,
 And calls the raptures to her plenteous face.
 What numbers for those charming features pine,
 If blooming acres round her temples twine!
 Her lip the strawberry, and her eyes more bright
10 Than sparkling Venus in a frosty night;
 Pale lilies fade and, when the fair appears,
 Snow turns a negro and dissolves in tears,
 And, where the charmer treads her magic toe,
 On English ground Arabian odours grow;
 Till mighty Hymen lifts his sceptred rod,
 And sinks her glories with a fatal nod,
 Dissolves her triumphs, sweeps her charms away,
 And turns the goddess to her native clay.

VIII フェミニズムの詩

　女とは，愛敬はあるが短命の花，
柔弱すぎて仕事に向かず，虚弱にすぎて力なく，
妻になれば奴隷の身，そうでなければオールドミスよ，
醜ければ蔑まれ，美しければ騙される．
富だけが優雅さすべてを呼び起こし
顔も豊かに有頂天．
あの魅力ある目鼻立ちに恋い焦がれる者は数知れぬ，
花盛りの広がりがこめかみ周りを取り巻けば！
唇はいちご，両の眼はきらきらと
霜夜の金星よりも輝き光る．　　　　　　　　　　　　　　10
青白い百合の花は色褪せ，美女が出てくれば，
雪も黒ん坊となり，涙に解ける，
そして妖婦が魅惑の踊りを舞うときは
イギリスの地にアラビアの香りが漂う．
だが遂に強大な結婚のハイメンがその王笏を持ち上げて，
女の栄光を殺しの一顧で沈めてしまう，
勝利の色も消え失せて，魅力もさっと逃げてゆき，
さしもの女神も元の土くれ．

　ここで女性解放思想の推移を少し概観しておこう．これまでにもフェミニズム的詩文が散見されないわけではなかった．例えば，Defoe (1660-1731) が堂々と自らの名前を署名した処女作『企画論』(*An Essay on Projects*, 1697) の中で，女子教育の必要性を論じているし，[5] 女ピカロの小説 *Moll Flanders* (1722) にも フェミニズム的解釈が充分に可能であろう．時に女嫌いともされる Swift (1667-1745) が愛する女

性 'Stella' や 'Vanessa' に対し，男女平等の友愛の詩を書いてもいる.[6] また Richardson (1689-1761) にしても，その小説 *Pamela* (1740) や *Clarissa* (1747-8) が男性の横暴や家父長制に対する批判と読めなくはない.

それはともかく，前述した18世紀初頭の Lady Chudleigh や Mary Leapor の時代から，女性の能力を蔑視し，もっぱら家事や技芸に閉じ込める男性の偏見と専横に抗し，ようやく女性たちは自らの置かれた境遇を自覚し，その不当性に抗議する気運が生じたのである．従来の伝統的な理想的女性像，すなわち繊細な感情や洗練された趣味を持つだけの「炉端の天使」ではすまなくなった.

世紀半ばには，女性にも有用な知識や学問の習得を促す教育の重要性が次第に叫ばれるようになり，いわゆる青鞜派の女性たち，即ち Elizabeth Montagu (1720-1800) を始めとして，Elizabeth Carter (1717-1806), Hester Chapone (1727-1801), Hannah More (1745-1833) らが主に活発な文学活動を行なうに至った.

このような女性解放運動を集大成するかのように，Wollstonecraft (1759-97) が『女性の権利の擁護』(*A Vindication of the Rights of Woman*, 1792) によって，本格的なフェミニズムの暁鐘を打ち鳴らしたのである．19世紀に入っても，リチャードソンの膨大な書簡集を編んだ才女 Anna Laetitia Barbauld (1743-1825) は，ウルストンクラーフトに呼応して，'The Rights of Woman' (*c.* 1795; 1825)[7] の冒頭第一行を次のように書いた.

'Yes, injured Woman! assert thy right!'

注

1) *18th W P*, No.2, p.3.
2) 当時の女性の地位の状況一般については，本書の「序」に挙げた次の2点が参考になろう．

Feminism in Eighteenth-Century England, ed. Katherine M. Rogers (University of Illinois Press, 1982).

Eighteenth-Century Women: An Anthology, ed. Bridget Hill (London, 1984).これには次の翻訳がある．福田良子訳，ブリジェット・ヒル『女性たちの十八世紀』－イギリスの場合－（みすず書房，1990）．

なお，女性作家論として次の参考書を挙げておく．Cheryl Turner, *Living by the Pen: Women Writers in the Eighteenth Century* (1992; London and New York: Routledge, 1994).

3) *18th W P*, No.140, pp. 211-2.
4) *New 18th V*, No.269, pp. 408-9.

本格的なフェミニズムへの橋渡し役の一つ，Mary Scott の522行から成る長詩 *The Female Advocate; A Poem. Occasioned by Reading Mr. Duncombe's Feminead* (1774) には，次のような一節 (ll. 21-24) がある．

Whilst LORDLY MAN asserts his right divine,
Alone to bow at wisdom's sacred shrine;
With tyrant sway would keep the female mind
In error's cheerless dark abyss confin'd?

殿様ぶった男性が神授の権利と主張して，
ひとり知恵の聖堂にぬかずいて，

女性の心をいつまでも横暴に支配して
迷妄の侘しい奈落に閉じ込めるのか？
(*The Augustan Reprint Society*, No.224, 1984)

　しかし結論的には，男性に伍して学問や知識を求め，精神的な向上を目指しながらも，「家庭の天使」と両立する才女の道を志向している詩のように思われる．

　なお，次の通り S. F. (Sarah Fige) によるこれと同題の女性風刺に対する弁護論がある．既に前世紀以来，このような女性批判がやがてフェミニズムを醸成する温床となるのであろう．*The Female Advocate: Or, an Answer to a Late Satyr against the Pride, Lust and Inconstancy of Woman. Written by a Lady in Vindication of her Sex. Licens'd, June 2, 1686* (1687)
(*The Augustan Reprint Society,* No.180, 1976)

5) 'The Education of Women' in *Century Readings in English Literature,* ed. Cunliffe, Young, Van Doren (1910; New York: Appleton-Century-Crofts, Inc, 1940), Fifth Edition, pp.408-9.

6) 拙著『スウィフトの詩』(九州大学出版会，1993)，三　スウィフトの「ステラ詩」－友情とフェミニズムを中心に－，pp.115-51.

7) Margaret Ferguson, Mary Jo Salter. Jon Stallworthy, eds., *The Norton Anthology of Poetry* (1970; W.W.Norton & Company, 1996). Fourth Edition, pp.646-7.

IX 続フェミニズムの詩

1 Ann Murry, 'The Tête à Tête, Or Fashionable Pair. An Eclogue'

　もちろん当時の女性詩がすべて急進的なフェミニズム一辺倒というわけではない．その主張にも当然，濃淡や深浅のバリエーションがあった．即ち，大別すれば，真正面から社会・経済・宗教の諸制度，特に婚姻法などの改革に立ち向かう先鋭な立場もあれば，また自己教育を通して個人的に目覚めようとしつつ，妻や母として家庭的配慮を忘れぬ立場もあった．

　ここでは，次のように余裕ある上流貴族社会の夫妻，その名も Sir Charles Modish と Lady Modish の間に交わされる「牧歌」的対話に耳を傾けてみよう．ぶどう酒商人の娘ながら，教育を受け，勤勉に家庭教師として生計を立てたアン・マリ (*c.* 1755—after1816) 24才頃の作といわれる「打ち解けた対話，あるいは当世風夫妻，一つの牧歌」(1779)[1] と題する137行がそれである．

The Tête à Tête, Or Fashionable Pair. An Eclogue

[SIR CHARLES MODISH and LADY MODISH]

SIR C. My dear! this morning we will take a ride,
   And call on Lord Rupee, and Lady Pride.

LADY M. With all my heart; and bring them home to dine:
   I like the scheme, the weather is so fine.
   Sir Charles! now read the news: pray, who is dead?
   And see if Lady Jane is brought to bed.

SIR C. The last new tragedy is well received;
   And Harrison, I see, is clear reprieved;
   Good Captain Bluster has obtained a Flag:
   I hope he will promote Lieutenant Brag!
   Where is my chocolate? The toast is cold.
   Lord Squander's pictures are, I find, just sold.

LADY M. Indeed, I feared his fortune was deranged;
   Of late his countenance was vastly changed;
   Like a barometer, the face explains
   The fall and rise of our uncertain gains.

SIR C. He was good-natured, and a well-bred man,
   Yet seemed surrounded with a dangerous clan.
   Tomorrow I'm resolved to go to town,
   To settle that affair with Captain Brown.

IX 続フェミニズムの詩

Sir C. ねえお前! 今朝は遠出をしよう．
 そしてルビー卿とプライド夫人を訪ねよう．

Lady M. 喜んで，そしてお食事に家へ呼びましょう．
 いい計画ですわ，天気は上々ですし．
 あなた! いまニュースを読んで下さいな．ねぇ，どなたが亡くなったの?
 それとジェイン様お産をなさるのかしら．

Sir C. この前の新しい悲劇は好評だ．
 そしてハリソンは，どうやら執行猶予だね．
 ブラスター大佐が艦長になった，
 ブラグ大尉を上げて欲しいもんだ!
 わしのチョコレートはどこだ? トーストが冷えた．
 スクウォンダー卿の絵が，ちょうど売れたようだ．

Lady M. ほんとに，あの方の運勢左前と気がかりでした，
 最近あの顔色が随分変わりましたもの，
 バロメーターみたいに，顔で分かります
 わたしたちの不確かな儲けの上がり下がりは．

Sir C. あの男は好人物で育ちがよかった，
 だがどうやら回りがちょっと危ない一族でね．
 明日は上京に決めた．
 ブラウン大佐とあの一件を片付けにな．

LADY M. And leave me quite alone in this dull place!
    Whilst you are gone, to see no human face!
    This dreary season gaiety best suits;
    'Tis hard to spend my time with rustic brutes.

SIR C. No cause but business e'er could make me leave
    Your Ladyship, whose absence I shall grieve;
    But really, our expenses are so great,
    To keep up the parade of useless state,
    'Tis needful for to live a rural life,
30   Though with my inclination oft at strife.
    My steward plagues me with his loud complaint,
    Enough to tire the patience of a saint,
    With such a catalogue of human ills,
    Repairs, subscriptions, and long tradesmen's bills;
    The land-tax is so high, the stocks so low,
    And for my credit, 'tis, alas—so so!
    Though hard my lot, I must avoid a worse,
    And e'en consent to put m' estate to nurse.

LADY M. How cruel is my fate! how great the fall!
40   So large my fortune, yet my jointure small.
    Then my precedence is, alas! so low,
    That even citizens before me go:
    A Lady-Mayoress e'en as good as me,
    Though her weak husband may retail bohea.

Lady M. それでこんな退屈な所にわたしを独りぼっち
   になさるの!
　お留守の間, 人っ子ひとり会えないのですよ!
　こんな侘しい季節は賑やかなのが一番なのに,
　無骨な田舎者と過ごすのはご免ですわ.

Sir C. 仕事ででもなければ独りで出かけたりはしないさ
　お前を置いて, わしだってお前がいないと淋しいからな.
　だが実際, 我々の費用はばかにならないんだ,
　やたら豪勢なところを見せびらかすとな,
　田舎暮らしをするのが必要なんだ,
　わしの性分とはあんまり折り合わぬのだが.
　執事が大声で不平を言うのも困ったもんだ,
　上人(しょうにん)様でも堪忍袋の緒が切れよう,
　一連のあんな不幸がいろいろ続き,
　修繕やら, 予約講読やら, 長期の商人手形やら.
　地租がとっても高く, 株価はとっても低い,
　それにわしの信用は, 悲しいことに —— まあそこそこ!
　運勢は厳しいが, これ以上悪くはしないようにせねば
   ならん,
　所領は管財人に任せることに同意をしてもな.

Lady M. わたしの運は何とひどいこと! 何と落ちぶれ
   たものでしょう!
　あんなに大きな財産だったのに, 寡婦財産が少なくなっ
   て.

それじゃわたしの席次は，まあ悲しい，とっても低くなって，
庶民にすら晴れの場で先を越されるわ，
市長夫人だってわたしと同等なのに，
尤もあの方の弱いご亭主は中国紅茶の小売りをなさるけど．

SIR C. Nay, pray my Lady! cease to be so loud,
　　Nor of your consequence be yet so proud;
　　The fortune which you boast was basely won,
　　And by your father's gains Lord George undone.
　　Women of highest rank so thoughtless live,
50　　They naught but sorrow and vexation give;
　　In dissipated scenes they spend their time,
　　Infants in sense, thought oft in years past prime.

LADY M. In vain, Sir Charles! you strive my heart to vex;
　　I will revere and vindicate my sex.
　　Deign but to ask where female grace is seen,
　　I thus reply—in our benignant Queen!
　　In her, the mother and the wife we find,
　　Blended with majesty, and sense refined:
　　Blest with a Monarch's love, a nation's praise,
60　　Her worth transcendent shall adorn my lays;
　　Not Faction's venom can her power disown,

IX 続フェミニズムの詩

Or Slander tarnish her illustrious throne.
From Royal George a bright example take,
As good an husband and a father make,
And strive like him no ordinance to break.

SIR C. Your Ladyship, with wond'rous skill and might,
Brings strong conviction for to act aright:
Be thou what Charlotte is, and then my heart
Sure cannot fail to act a George's part.

Sir C. いや，お願いだ! そんな大声はやめてくれ,
　それにまたそんなに自分を偉いと誇ってはならん,
　お前の自慢の財産は卑劣な手段で手に入れた,
　そうしてお前の父親の儲けでジョージ卿は破産した.
　上流の婦人たちがそんな軽率な暮らしぶりだから,
　悲しみと苛立ちしか与えない. 50
　ご婦人連は放埓な社交場裏で日を送る,
　分別は幼児なみ, 歳はたいてい盛りを過ぎて.

Lady M. 駄目よ, あなた! 怒らせようとなさっても,
　わたしは同性を大事に弁護しますわ.
　女性の奥床しさがどこにあるとお尋ねなら,
　こう答えます ── 優しい女王様に, と!
　あの方こそ, 母であり妻であり,
　威厳と優雅さが解け合って,
　王様の愛と, 国民の称賛を受けられ,

60　　　その並はずれた価値がわたしの歌を飾ります．
　　　党派の毒舌もお后の力は否めませんし，
　　　中傷も輝く王座を汚せません．
　　　国王ジョージから立派な手本を学び，
　　　同じくらい良い夫，よい父となり，
　　　神の掟を破らぬように同じようにお努めなさい．

Sir C. お前は素晴らしい説得力で，
　　　正しく振舞う確信を与えてくれる．
　　　お前は后のシャーロット様のようになれ，そうすれば
　　　わしの心は
　　　必ずやジョージの役が果たせるよ．

70　　LADY M. Pray now, Sir Charles! explain your present view,
　　　And for the children what will you pursue?

　　SIR C. As for the girls, I'll send them all to France,
　　　Where they will learn to chatter French, and dance:
　　　But if you like it better, or as well,
　　　I'll have at home a modern Mad'moiselle.
　　　The boys I mean to thrive by trade or law;
　　　And bring them up with due respect and awe.
　　　Charles, who I think is something like an ass,
　　　May do, perhaps, at Bombay or Madras.

IX 続フェミニズムの詩

LADY M. In Britain bred, in Britain freely born,　　80
　A foreign education hence I scorn.
　Will foreign teachers English minds expand,
　And point the beauties of our native land?
　Will they not strive to alienate the heart,
　And gain new proselytes with laboured art?
　Will they not deem it heresy to teach
　Minds that have fled from Superstition's reach?
　Knowledge so gained is purchased much too dear;
　Such measures I oppose, with heart sincere.
　The boys, I trust, by industry will rise,　　90
　And all be happy, fortunate, or wise;
　As for poor Charles, I can't endure the plan,
　Though rich as Croesus, or as Kouli Khan;
　I hate a Nabob's great and ill-got wealth,
　Bought at th' expense of peace and precious health;
　If they return with treasures vast of gold,
　Conscience upbraids them, nor e'er quits her hold;
　The poisoned dagger, and the tainted bowl,
　Are ever present to the guilty soul:
　Remember Harpax, thy unhappy friend,　　100
　How splendid was his life!—how sad his end!

Lady M. では，あなた！今のお考えをご説明遊ばせ，　　70
　子供たちのためにどんな事をなさいます？

Sir C. 娘たちについては，皆フランスに送ろう，
そこでフランス語を喋りダンスを覚えるだろう．
しかし，もっと上策を望むなら，いや同じくらいか，
邸にモダンな女性の家庭教師を雇い入れよう．
息子らは貿易か法律で成功するように，
それ相応の配慮をもって育てよう．
チャールズは少々抜けているようだが，
まあボンベイかマドラスでやっていけよう．

80 Lady M. イギリス育ち，イギリスで不自由ない生まれですから，
外国の教育をわたしは軽蔑します．
外国の教師たちがイギリス精神を発展させて，
わたしたち母国の美しさを示してくれるでしょうか？
むしろ心を余所に向けようとして，
手のこんだ細工で新たに改宗させるのではありませんこと？
あの教師たちは異端だと考えないのでは，
逆に迷信を素直な心に吹き込んだりして？
そうして得た知識は余りに高過ぎる買物，
そんな手段には反対します，心の底から．
90 息子たちは，勤勉なら出世すると信じます，
そして皆，幸せで，運よく，また賢くなるでしょう．
チャールズのことは，可哀相で，わたしその計画に耐えられません．
クロイソスのように，またクリ・カーンのように金持ちでも，

IX 続フェミニズムの詩   127

インド帰りのお大尽の不正の富は嫌いです，
平穏と大切な健康を犠牲にして購うのでしたら．
莫大な金の宝を持ち帰っても，
良心が咎め，また心の痛みが取れません．
毒を塗った剣や毒杯が
いつも疚しい魂に浮かんできます．
あなたの不幸な友人，ハーパックスさんのことをお忘れにならないで，   100
何と素晴らしい人生だったことでしょう！── でも何と悲しい結末！

SIR C. You think too closely, weigh each point and grain,

　Which ill accords with more substantial gain.

　As for myself, a Patriot I will turn,

　Yet for my private good with ardour burn;

　Oppose the Minister in all his views,

　And make my fortune in the way I choose.

LADY M. Fictitious Patriots are a fixed disgrace,

　And found too oft but statesmen out of place;

　Like Reynard in the fable, gasp for power,   110

　And only yelp because the grapes are sour.

　For Liberty they roar like idle boys,

　Which they misuse as children do their toys.

　Licentious freedom is the gift they ask,

Which wears, sweet Liberty! thy pleasing mask.

SIR C. But list! I think I hear the children's noise:
How I am plagued with chattering girls and boys!

LADY M. To you, I must confess, their infant sounds
Are not so pleasing as your dice and hounds.
Sir Charles, I wonder you dislike their talk;
Their opening reason you oppress and balk.

SIR C. The nursery's best suited to their plays,
I hate the fuss of all their childish ways;
At meals especially I will be quiet,
And where they are, there is perpetual riot.

LADY M. Alas! you hate the matrimonial life,
Domestic joys, and e'en your faithful wife;
Your children are a burthen, and your home
A cheerless place, and melancholy dome.

SIR C. I never will forgo the joys of life
To please the haughty or capricious wife.
The man who lets a thoughtless woman rule
Must needs be deemed a most egregious fool.
My future prospects I resign to chance,
And for the present will retire to France;

　　　　IX　続フェミニズムの詩　　　　　　129

The remedy you'll gain in legal course:
A separate stipend, or a kind divorce.

　　　　　　　　　　　　　　　　（1779）

Sir C. お前はあんまり念入りに考え過ぎだ, いちいち
　細かいことを秤にかける,
　それではもっと実のある利益にそぐわない.
　わしの方は, 憂国の士になるが,
　でも内輪の幸福は熱を入れて求めるぞ.
　大臣の考えにはみな反対し,
　自分で選ぶ遣り方で運命を拓いてみせる.

Lady M. 仮想の愛国者気取りは恥の固まりで,
　ただ失意の政治家ってことがよくあるわ.
　寓話の狐のように, 権力を欲しがるくせに,
　ぶどうが酸っぱいからと吠えるだけ.
　自由のためと怠け坊主のように怒鳴るのです,
　子供の玩具のように自由を弄ぶのです.
　気ままな自由があの人たちの欲しいもの,
　それが, 美しい自由よ, お前の快い仮面をつけるのです.

Sir C. だが, ちょっと待て! 子供らの騒ぎが聞こえるぞ,
　娘や坊主らのぺちゃくちゃにはうんざりだ!

Lady M. あなたには, 正直に言いますが, あの子たち

の幼い声は
賭事や狩猟のように楽しくないのです.
120　あなた，どうして子供たちの話がお嫌いなんでしょう.
せっかく目覚めかけた物心をあなたは抑えて挫こうと
なさる.

Sir C. 子供部屋が彼らの遊びには一番よいのだ,
彼らの幼稚な空騒ぎはわしは嫌いだ.
食事では特に静かにするぞ,
子供らはどこでも，ひっきりなしの騒動だ.

Lady M. 悲しいわ，あなたは結婚生活がお嫌いなのね,
家庭的な喜びや，あなたの忠実な妻すらも.
子供たちが重荷で，あなたの家庭は
楽しくないところ，そして憂欝な家なのです.

130　Sir C. わしは決して人生の喜びを捨てはせん,
高慢なまた移り気な女房の機嫌をとったりして.
思慮のない女の言いなりになるような男は
途方もない大馬鹿者だとどうしたって考えねばならん.
わしの将来のことは運に任せて,
さしあたりフランスに隠退することにする.
救済策のことは法の手続きを踏んでお前のものになろう.
別途の給付金とか，寛大な離婚とか.

このように、この対話詩は、一見、田舎に住む上流階級夫妻の近隣の交際、世間話や新聞ダネ、劇評、女性論議、子供の躾や教育、政治向きの話題にまで及んで、当時のさまざまな世相を反映してはいるが、決して気楽な「牧歌」には終わっていない。やはり、消極的ながら亭主関白の夫への不服従という妻の目覚めが底流にあって、平凡な日常の陰に、夫婦の意見の対立から結婚生活の深刻な危機を孕んでいるのではなかろうか。つまり、女性の立場から見た上流社会の一断面が生き生きと語られていることになろう。

2 Jane West, 'To a Friend on her Marriage'

もう一篇、独学で13才から詩作を始め、近隣の自作農と結婚して3人の息子を育てたというジェイン・ウェスト（1758-1852）の「友人の結婚に際して」（1784）[2] から、その一部66行を抜いてみよう。

from *To a Friend on her Marriage, 1784*

MARRIED, poor soul! your empire's over;
Adieu the duteous kneeling lover;
Farewell, eternally farewell,
The glory of the stately belle;
The plumèd head, the trailing gown,
The crowded ball, the busy town,
For one short month are yours, and then
Must never be resumed again;

No more attentive Strephon flies,
10　Awed by the lightning of your eyes;
No longer, 'Madam, hear my vows,
But 'Mend this ragged wristband, spouse;
I mean to call upon a friend,
Do you your household cares attend.'
'Mayn't I go too, my dear?'— 'Oh, Lord!
What, married women go abroad!
Your horse is lame, the roads are rough,
Besides, at home you've work enough.'
Off goes the husband, brisk and airy;
20　The wife in a profound quandary,
Whilst he of wit or scandal chatters,
Remains mumchance, and darns old tatters.

　結婚したら，可哀相に！　あなたの帝国はおしまいよ．
従順に跪く恋人よ，さようなら．
去らば，永遠に去らば，
威厳ある美女の栄光よ．
羽根飾りの頭，裾引くガウン，
人の込み合う舞踏会，賑やかな町が
短い1か月はあなたのもの，そしてそれからは
2度と再び取り返しはつきません．
よく気が付くストレフォンももはや飛び回りはしない，
10　あなたの眼の雷光に畏れをなして．
もはや「ねえ君，僕の誓いを聞いて」ではなく，

IX 続フェミニズムの詩

「このほころびた袖口を繕ってくれ, お前.
友人を訪ねるつもりなんだ,
お前は家事に精出してくれ」となる.
「わたしも行ってはいけませんの, あなた?」── 「お お, まさか!
そんな, 結婚した女が外を出歩くなんぞ!
お前の馬は足が悪いし, 道路がひどい,
それに, 家にはたっぷり仕事があろう」
さっと夫は出かけ, 身も軽々と威勢よく,
妻はまったく途方に暮れて, 20
夫が洒落や噂の最中に,
無言のままで, ぼろを繕う.

　I almost think the nuptial hour
Possessed of talismanic power;
For in a little time, how strange,
We grow enamoured of the change.
Our tables and our chairs, in fact,
Possess perfections which attract,
Till, like the snail, we gladly bear
The constant weight of household care; 30
The things are trifles which we leave,
For trifles none but triflers grieve.
Like insects of the summer sky,
Were we but born to sport and die,
Then might we spread our gilded plumes,

And court the flower that sweetest blooms;
But heaven, which gave us nobler powers,
With ample duties filled our hours;
These shrink from solitary life
40 To grace the faithful active wife;
Her breast each social virtue warms,
Her mind each useful science charms;
Pleased, when she walks abroad, to hear
The orphan's thanks, the poor man's prayer;
Whene'er she makes the social call,
Her neighbour meets her in the hall,
And cries, 'I'm glad to see you come,
You really grow too fond of home':
That home, well ordered, proves her merit,
50 She is its animating spirit.
Each servant, at the task assigned,
Proclaims a regulating mind.
Pleased she surveys her infant charge,
Beholds the mental powers enlarge,
And as the young ideas rise,
Directs their issues to the skies.
Thus whilst performing Martha's part,
To serve the master of her heart,
How sweet the thought, that he approves,
60 Silent esteems, and deeply loves!

IX 続フェミニズムの詩

　わたしはほとんどこう思う，婚礼の時は
不思議な魔力を持つものと．
だってちょっとの間に，なんという不思議，
わたしたち変わった身分に夢中になって，
わたしらの机，わたしらの椅子が，ほんとに，
申し分なく立派に見えて心を惹かれ，
とうとう蝸牛のように，喜んで担いでしまう
家政という絶え間ない重荷を．　　　　　　　　　　　　　　30
わたしらが手放す物は取るに足りぬもの，
取るに足りぬ物を嘆くのは取るに足りぬ人．
夏空の虫のように，
わたしらが遊び戯れ死ぬためだけに生まれるのなら，
それならけばけばしい羽根を拡げて，
香り高く咲く花に言い寄ることができましょう．
でも天は，もっと高貴な力を下さって，
あり余る務めでわたしらの時間を満たされた．
この務めがあればこそ孤独な生活が避けられて
まめに働く妻に花を添えるのです．　　　　　　　　　　　　40
彼女の胸は人付き合いのたび暖まり，
彼女の心は役に立つ学問のたびうっとりとする．
嬉しいことに，外を歩けば，耳にする
孤児の感謝，貧しい人の祈り．
彼女が社交に訪ねればいつも，
隣人は玄関に出迎えて，
こう叫ぶ「よくお出かけ下さいました，
ほんとに家庭がお好きになられますよ」

家庭とは，よく整うと，妻の功績，
50　妻は家庭に生気を吹き込む霊なのです．
召使はそれぞれ，割り当てられた仕事で
規律を守る心を示す．
いそいそと妻は幼児の養育に配慮して，
知能が伸びるのを見守るのです．
そうして未熟な考えが起こるときは，
その結着を天に任せる．
こうしてマルタの役を果たしながら，
心に思う主人に仕える，
なんと快いことか，主人から認められ，
60　口には出さぬ敬意と，深い愛情を知ることは！

　Joy then, my Sally, since I see
The path of wedlock trod by thee;
Thy virtues shall secure the palm,
Hymeneal friendship's placid calm,
And show to a too polished nation
Example worthy imitation.

(Wr. 1784; pub. 1799)

　だから喜びなさい，わたしのサリーよ，わたしには見える
あなたの歩む結婚の道が．
あなたの美徳は勝利の棕櫚(しゅろ)を手に入れる，
結婚の友情の穏やかな平穏を．
そうして示しておあげ，垢抜け過ぎた国民に

真似るに足る範例を．

　こう読んでくると，この詩はフェミニスト的発想ながら，論旨は次第に伝統的な女性のあるべき姿へと移り，遂には家庭的義務への献身を説き，模範的な妻や母としての婦徳を薦める結びとなっている．この女流詩人は慎ましい生まれ育ちを反映してか，宗教心も厚く，当時のフェミニズム風潮の中にあっての保守派ということになろうか．あながちフェミニスト崩れとは言わないでおこう．世は既に 'Feminism' から 'Femininity' へ向かう兆しを見せているのかもしれない．

注

1)　*18th WP*, No.233, pp. 357-61.
2)　Ibid., No.250, pp. 380-2.

なお全般的に，初期から現代に至る約400人の女流作家の生涯や作品を概観したものとして，次の参考書が便利である．　*The Oxford Guide to British Women Writers,* edited by Joanne Shattock (1993; rpt, Oxford University Press paperback, 1994).

X 社会派の詩

1 Hannah More, 'Slavery, A Poem'

女性詩も世紀が進むにつれ，日常卑近な家庭生活や結婚の問題だけでなく，広く内外の情勢を反映して社会的関心を見せるようになった．その一例として，青鞜派の有力メンバーで Johnson グループの文人たちとも親しかったハナ・モア（1745-1833）の「奴隷制，一つの詩」(*Slavery, A Poem*, 1788)[1] から，その 44 行を取り上げてみたい．モア女史は，ウルストンクラーフトのように必ずしも女性の権利を主張せず，むしろ伝統的な婦徳，教育，宗教，慈善や貧民救済などを重視し，奴隷廃止運動に尽力した慈善家 William Wilberforce（1759-1833）の友人であったことを付言しておこう．

from *Slavery, A Poem*

Perish th' illiberal thought which would debase
The native genius of the sable race!
Perish the proud philosophy, which sought
To rob them of the powers of equal thought!
Does then th' immortal principle within

X 社会派の詩　　　　　139

Change with the casual colour of the skin?
Does matter govern spirit? or is mind
Degraded by the form to which 'tis joined?

　滅ぼしてしまえ,その狭量な考えを
黒人の生来の天稟を卑しめるではないか!
滅ぼしてしまえ傲慢な哲学,それこそが
彼等から平等の力を奪おうとしたのだ!
一体,内なる不滅の本質が
たまたま肌の色の違いで変わるのか?
肉体が霊を支配するのか?　それとも精神は
それが結びつけられる形相(けいそう)によって貶められるのか?

　No: they have heads to think, and hearts to feel,
And souls to act with firm, though erring, zeal;　　　　10
For they have keen affections, kind desires,
Love strong as death, and active patriot fires;
All the rude energy, the fervid flame,
Of high-souled passion, and ingenuous shame:
Strong but luxuriant virtues boldly shoot
From the wild vigour of a savage root.
　Nor weak their sense of honour's proud control,
For pride is virtue in a pagan soul;
A sense of worth, a conscience of desert,
A high, unbroken haughtiness of heart:　　　　20
That self-same stuff which erst proud empires

swayed,
Of which the conquerors of the world were made.
Capricious fate of man! that very pride
In Afric scourged, in Rome was deified....

　否，彼等には考える頭があり，感ずる心がある，
10　そして間違っても，揺がぬ情熱で行動する魂がある．
だって彼等にはある，激しい情愛，優しい願い，
死のごとく強い愛，そして活発な愛国心の火が，
あらゆる逞しいエネルギー，燃えるような焔，
高潔な情熱の，純真な羞恥の．
強いが豊かな徳が大胆に芽を出すのだ
野性の根の荒々しい活力から．
　また弱からず，彼等の自尊心からくる誇らかな抑制も，
誇りこそは異教の魂の美徳なのだから．
価値観，道義心，
高く，挫けぬ勇猛な心，
20　かつて誇り高い帝国を支配したあの同じ素質，
そこから世界の征服者たちは作られた．
人間の移り気な運命よ！その誇りそのものが
アフリカで鞭打たれ，ローマで崇められた‥‥

And thou, White Savage! whether lust of gold,
Or lust of conquest, rule thee uncontrolled!
Hero, or robber! ─ by whatever name
Thou plead thy impious claim to wealth or fame;

X 社会派の詩   141

Whether inferior mischiefs be thy boast,
A petty tyrant rifling Gambia's coast: 30
Or bolder carnage track thy crimson way,
Kings dispossessed, and provinces thy prey;
Panting to tame wide earth's remotest bound,
All Cortez murdered, all Columbus found;
O'er plundered realms to reign, detested lord,
Make millions wretched, and thyself abhorred;—
In Reason's eye, in Wisdom's fair account,
Your sum of glory boasts a like amount;
The means may differ, but the end's the same:
Conquest is pillage with a nobler name. 40
Who makes the sum of human blessings less,
Or sinks the stock of general happiness,
No solid fame shall grace, no true renown
His life shall blazon, or his memory crown.

(1788)

　そして汝, 白き野蛮人よ！　黄金欲か
はたまた征服欲か, 汝を抑えがたく支配するのはいずれか！
英雄か, 盗賊か！── いかなる名前にても
汝は富か名誉に神を畏れぬ権利を主張する.
卑劣な危害が汝の自慢であるにせよ,
けちな暴君がガンビアの岸辺を荒らそうと, 30
あるいは更に大胆不敵な殺戮が汝の深紅の道を辿ろうと,
諸王が廃位され, 諸領地が汝の餌食になろうとも,

広い地球の果ての果てまで服従させようと喘いで,
コルテスが皆殺しを行なおうとも,コロンブスが何処を発見しようとも,
掠奪した領土で君臨しようとも,唾棄すべき領主よ,
幾百万の人々を惨めにし,己は憎悪の的となる,──
理性の眼,叡智の公正な評価では,
お前がどれだけ栄光を集めても,その自慢の高は知れたもの,
手段は違っても,目的は同じこと.
40 征服は名が一段と高い略奪だ.
人間の幸せの総量を更に少なく減じたり,
世の幸福の蓄えを減らす者は,
いかなる真の名誉にも飾られず,いかなる真実の栄誉にもその人生は飾られず,またその追憶に花が添えられることはない.

　このように,この一節によっても,さすがにウィルバフォースを直接に知る人だけあって,この青鞜派の才女は,当時の奴隷に対する白人たちの迫害,野蛮な征服や収奪を厳しく糾弾していることが分かるであろう.ちなみに,ほぼ百年前,イギリス最初の女流作家 Aphra Behn は奴隷売買に抗議した小説 *Oroonoko* (1688)で,「高貴な野蛮人」('the noble savage')を描いていた.[2)]

　2　Helen Maria Williams, 'To Dr. Moore, in Answer to a Poetical Epistle Written by Him in Wales'

X 社会派の詩

　次は,フランス革命に熱中した急進主義者ヘレン・マライア・ウィリアムズ (1761?-1827) の詩を見よう.「ムーア博士へ,ウェールズにて書かれた彼の詩的書簡に答えて」(1792)[3] と題する 4 連の 96 行の長詩である. 彼女はウェールズ出身の陸軍将校を父に持ち,その死後は母親に教育され,文壇で成功を収め,フランスに渡っては,やはり急進派の Thomas Paine (1737-1809) やウルストンクラーフトと知り合い,フランス革命を直接に目撃して,ジロンド党のリーダーとも親しく,ロベスピエールによって投獄され危うく処刑寸前の体験もした女性であった.

To Dr. Moore, in Answer to a Poetical Epistle
Written by Him in Wales

[*On the French Revolution*]

　W<small>HILE</small> in long exile far from you I roam,
To soothe my heart with images of home,
For me, my friend, with rich poetic grace
The landscapes of my native isle you trace;
Her cultured meadows, and her lavish shades,
Her winding rivers, and her verdant glades;
Far as where, frowning on the flood below,
The rough Welsh mountain lifts its craggy brow;
Where nature throws aside her softer charms,
And with sublimer views the bosom warms.　　10

144

　長らく流浪して貴方から遠く離れている間に,
故郷のイメージで私の心を慰めようと,
私のために, わが友よ, 詩情豊かに
私の生まれた島国の景色を描いて下さる,
耕された牧草地, あり余る木陰,
曲がりくねる川, そして緑の林間の空き地,
遠く, 眼下の流れを睨んで
峨々たるウェールズの山がその岩だらけの顔を上げるところ,
自然が一段と穏やかな魅力を見捨てて,
10　一段と雄大な眺めで心を温めてくれるところ.

　Meanwhile my steps have strayed where Autumn yields
A purple harvest on the sunny fields;
Where, bending with their luscious weight, recline
The loaded branches of the clustering vine;
There, on the Loire's sweet banks, a joyful band
Culled the rich produce of the fruitful land;
The youthful peasant and the village maid,
And feeble age and childhood lent their aid.
The labours of the mornnig done, they haste
20　Where the light dinner in the field is placed;
Around the soup of herbs a circle make,
And all from one vast dish at once partake:
The vintage-baskets serve, reversed, for chairs,

X 社会派の詩　　　　　　　　　　145

And the gay meal is crowned with tuneless airs;
For each in turn must sing with all his might,
And some their carols pour in nature's spite.

　さて，私はさ迷い歩いた，秋のさなか
日の当たる畑に紫色の収穫ができるところを．
そこでは甘美な重みでたわみながら，うなだれている
鈴なりの葡萄房の実をつけた枝．
そのロワール河の美しい土手で，楽しい一団が
肥えた土地の豊かな実りを摘み取った．
若い農夫と村の娘が，
か弱い年寄りや子供らが手を助けた．
朝の労働がすむと，彼等は急ぐ
野での軽い食事が置いてあるところへ．　　　　　　　　　　20
ハーブのスープの周りに輪を作り，
一つの大皿から皆が一斉に食事する．
葡萄かごが逆さになって椅子がわり，
賑やかな食事のあとは調子外れの唄で締めくくる，
ひとりひとり交替で力一杯歌うのが決まり，
なかにはクリスマスを祝う歌を季節外れにがなる者がいる．

　Delightful land! ah, now with general voice
Thy village sons and daughters may rejoice;
Thy happy peasant, now no more—a slave
Forbade to taste one good that nature gave—　　　　　　30
Views with the anguish of indignant pain

The bounteous harvest spread for him in vain.
Oppression's cruel hand shall dare no more
To seize with iron grip his scanty store,
And from his famished infants wring those spoils,
The hard-earned produce of his useful toils;
For now on Gallia's plains the peasant knows
Those equal rights impartial heaven bestows.
He now, by freedom's ray illumined, taught
40 Some self-respect, some energy of thought,
Discerns the blessings that to all belong,
And lives to guard his humble shed from wrong.

　楽しい里よ！　ああ，いま皆が声を合わせて
お前の村の息子や娘らは喜びを共にできる．
お前の幸せな農夫は，今もはや一奴隷
30 自然が恵む幸は何ひとつ味えず──
はらわたが煮えくり返る苦しみで眺めるのです，
豊かな収穫が自分には空しく広がるのを．
抑圧の酷薄な手でももはや犯しはすまい，
鉄の柄で彼の乏しい蓄えをつかみ，
飢えた幼な子らからあの成果をもぎ取ったりは，
汗水垂らして働いてやっと手に入れた産物だから．
だって今ガリアの野では農夫が知っている，
公平な天が授けるあの平等の権利のことを．
彼は今，自由の輝く光によって，教えた
40 ある者には自尊心を，ある者には思想の力を，

万人に属する恵みを見分け,
みすぼらしい陋屋を不正から守るために生きる.

  Auspicious Liberty! in vain thy foes
Deride thy ardour, and thy force oppose;
In vain refuse to mark thy spreading light,
While, like the mole, they hide their heads in night,
Or hope their eloquence with taper-ray
Can dim the blaze of philosophic day;
Those reasoners who pretend that each abuse,
Sanctioned by precedent, has some blest use!   50
Does then some chemic power to time belong,
Extracting by some process right from wrong?
Must feudal governments for ever last,
Those Gothic piles, the works of ages past?
Nor may obtrusive reason boldly scan,
Far less reform, the rude, mishapen plan?
The winding labyrinths, the hostile towers,
Whence danger threatens, and where horror lowers;
The jealous drawbridge, and the moat profound,
The lonely dungeon in the caverned ground;   60
The sullen dome above those central caves,
Where lives one despot and a host of slaves?—
Ah, Freedom, on this renovated shore
That fabric frights the moral world no more!
Shook to its basis by thy powerful spell,

Its triple walls in massy fragments fell;
While, rising from the hideous wreck, appears
The temple thy firm arm sublimely rears;
Of fair proportions, and of simple grace,
70 A mansion worthy of the human race.
For me, the witness of those scenes, whose birth
Forms a new era in the storied earth,
Oft, while with glowing breast those scenes I view,
They lead, ah friend beloved, my thoughts to you!
Ah, still each fine emotion they impart
With your idea mingles in my heart;
You, whose warm bosom, whose expanded mind,
Have shared this glorious triumph of mankind;
You, whom I oft have heard, with generous zeal,
80 With all that truth can urge or pity feel,
Refute the pompous argument, that tried
The common cause of millions to deride;
With reason's force the plausive sophist hit,
Or dart on folly the bright flash of wit;
Too swift, my friend, the moments winged their flight,
That gave at once instruction and delight;
That ever from your ample stores of thought
To my small stock some new accession brought.
How oft remembrance, while this bosom bleeds,
90 My pensive fancy to your dwelling leads;
Where, round your cheerful hearth, I weeping trace

X 社会派の詩　　　　　　　　　　149

The social circle, and my vacant place! —
When, to that dwelling friendship's tie endears,
When shall I hasten with the 'joy of tears'?
That joy whose keen sensation swells to pain,
And strives to utter what it feels, in vain.

　　　　　　　　　　　　　　　　（1792）

　めでたい自由よ！　お前の敵どもが
お前の熱意を嘲り，お前の力に逆らっても無駄だ，
お前の光が広がるのを認めまいとしても無駄だ．
一方，もぐらのように，彼等は頭を夜の闇に隠したり，
また彼等の雄弁がローソクの灯で
理性の昼の輝きをかげらせると期待する．
あの理論家たちの主張では，どんな濫用も
先例によって赦されれば，何か多少は役に立つ！　　　　50
とすれば，錬金術の力は時間に属するものか？
何かの操作で邪から正を引き出しながら．
封建的な政府が永遠に続かねばならぬのか，
あのゴシック建築群，過去の時代の産物が？
あるいはまた出しゃばりの理性が大胆に調べたり，
況んや改善はできぬのか，拙劣な不運な計画を？
曲がりくねった迷路，敵意のこもった塔，
油断のならぬ吊り上げ橋と深い濠，
穴を掘った寂しい土牢，　　　　　　　　　　　　　　60
あの主な洞窟の上の陰気なドーム，
一人の暴君と奴隷の群はどこに住んでいるのか？——

ああ，自由よ，この革新の岸辺で
あの建物はもはや精神世界を脅かしはしない！
お前の力強い魔力でその土台を揺さぶられ，
その三重の壁が大量の破片となって崩れた．
一方，その見るも恐ろしい廃墟から，立ち現れる
お前の引き締まった腕が高々と建てる神殿が，
見事な均整と，素朴な優美さを持ち，
70 　人類にふさわしい大邸宅が．
私としては，あの情景の目撃者，その出現こそが
歴史を刻む大地に新しい時代を作る．
しばしば胸を熱くしながらあの情景を見ていると，
ああ愛する友よ，私の想いは貴方のもとへ赴く！
ああ，今でもその情景が伝える素晴らしい感動がみな
私の心の中で貴方のことと混じり合う．
貴方は，その暖かい胸，その広い心で，
人類のこの輝かしい勝利を分かち合われた．
貴方は，しばしば耳にしたことだが，偏見のない熱意を
もって，
80 　真実に促され，哀れみを抱けるすべての人々とともに，
大げさな議論に反駁される，その狙いが
幾百万の人に共通な目的を嘲ろうとしたのだから．
理性の力で尤もらしい詭弁家を叩き，
愚行には機知の鮮やかな閃光を投げかけられる．
余りに早く，わが友よ，時が翼で飛び去った，
教訓と喜びを同時に与えてくれたものなのに．
いつも貴方の有り余る思想の蓄えから

私のささやかな在庫を新たに増やしていたものなのに．
幾度，想い出が，この胸が血の出るように痛むとき，
憂いに沈む心を貴方の住まいへ導くことか．   90
そこでは，貴方の楽しい炉の周りで，私は涙ながらに辿るのです
あの社交の輪と，私の居ない席を！——
いつになったら，友情の絆で慕わしいあの住まいへ，
いつになったら私は'涙の喜び'で急いで行けるのでしょうか？
あの喜びはその強烈な感覚が膨らんで苦痛となり，
それが感じるものをとても言い表わせはしないのです．

　このように，彼女はフランス革命の渦中にあって，自由，平等，友愛の理想に心酔しながらも，たまたま美しい秋の田園牧歌風景を前にして，望郷の念を絶ち難く，革命の共鳴者たるスコットランドの内科医ジョン・ムア（1729-1802）に宛てて，自己の政治的信念と感謝の書簡詩を認めたのである．

　だが，周知のごとく，革命の恐怖政治が進行するにつれ，Edmund Burke が『フランス革命の省察』(1790) で革命の非を警告したように，過激な破壊ではなく漸新的改革を説くイギリス保守主義の良識が支配的となった風潮の中で，飽くまで革命を支持して揺るがなかった彼女は，不倫の噂もあって，次第にイギリスの知人や理解者を失うに至ったのである．蛇足ながら，若きワーズワースが Axiologus の仮名でソネット 'Sonnet, On Seeing Miss Helen Maria Williams Weep at a Tale of Distress' (1787) を捧げていることを付け加えておこう．

3 Joseph Cottle, 'Malvern Hills'

次は当時 Bristol の本屋として有名で，*Lyrical Ballads*を出版したジョウゼフ・コットル（1770-1853）の「モールヴァン丘陵」(1798)[4)] を取り上げてみたい．この丘陵地帯は中世の Langland の *Piers the Plowman* ゆかりの地，イギリス南西部の鉱泉保養地でもある．初期の産業革命がこの地にもたらした災禍の一端を知ることができよう．

from *Malvern Hills*

[*Industrial Evils*]

CITIES and towns, ye haunts of wretchedness!
Where Commerce with a grin of ecstasy
Sits counting o'er her votaries' tears and sighs;
Urged by your splendid poisons, what a host
Of inexperienced sons have left their homes,
The cot's calm comforts and the quiet shades,
To taste your bitter dregs, and be immured
From morn's first dawn till evening far is spent,
In dust and stench and pestilence! remote
10   From friends, assailed by vice in every shape
That chains to dust the soul, and doomed at length
To linger out their blasted lives in scorn—
Their peace destroyed—their innocence gone by.

都市と町，お前たち惨めさの巣窟よ！

X 社会派の詩　　　　　　　　153

商業が恍惚の笑みを浮かべ
腰を下ろしてその信徒の涙と溜息を数え上げるところ,
お前たちの目もあやな毒に刺激され, 何と沢山の
未熟な息子らが家を出たことか,
田舎家の穏やかな楽しみと静かな木陰を捨てて,
お前たちの苦い残りかすを味わい, 閉じ込められるために,
朝早い曙から夜が更けるまで,
塵と臭いと悪疫の中に!　遠ざかる
友, あらゆる姿の悪徳に攻め立てられて　　　　　　　10
魂は埃に縛りつけられ, 終(つい)の定めは
枯れた命をだらだらと長引かせて蔑まれ——
彼等の平和は破壊され—— 彼等の無垢は跡形もない.

　Yet sadder still to mark the infant throng,
Foredoomed by Mammon's ironhearted sons
To deaths untimely, ere the simple lisp
Of infancy be past; to see them toil
And waste their tender strength, perchance to please
Some strict and pious master, who enjoys
Self-satisfaction in the cheering thought　　　　　　20
Of giving such unnumbered suppliants bread.
Cease, thoughtless men, your horrible deceits,
And, if to piety your heart incline,
Question it well! for never pious heart
Dwelt with such deeds. Can heaven applauding view
The helpless orphan seized by avarice,

And forced to sacrifice at Lucre's shrine
Its hopes in childhood and its joys in age?
No! if to please thy Maker ever struck
30 Thy passing thought, when interest was away,
Learn with more certainty than ever man
Foretold tomorrow's sun, it is by deeds
Of tenderness, by viewing all mankind
As offspring of one Sire, who never made
The wondrous human frame to be consumed,
Ere yet the leaves of childhood half expand,
By man's fierce lust of perishable gold.

　だが更に悲しいのは，幼児の群に目を止めるとき，
富の邪神の冷酷な息子らに予め運命を決められて
時ならぬ死の定め，頑是無いお喋りも
幼時の時代の済まぬうち．彼等の苦労を見るにつけ
か弱い力を浪費して，恐らくは喜ばせようと
厳しくて信心深い親方を，親方の楽しみは
20 自己満足の嬉しい想い
数知れぬあの嘆願者らにパンをやること．
止めよ，思慮なき人々よ，お前らの身の毛もよだつごまかしを，
そしてもしお前らの心が信心に傾けば，
よくそれを吟味せよ！　敬虔な心はついぞ
そんな行為に宿った例(ためし)がない．天が拍手喝采して眺められようか

X 社会派の詩　　　　　　　　　　155

無力な孤児が貪欲に捕らえられ,
マモンの社で犠牲とされるのを
幼時の希望と老令の喜びとを?
否! もし汝の造物主を喜ばせようと発心すれば
一時なりとも, 利害を離れ　　　　　　　　　　　　　　　　30
学ぶべし, かつて無きほど確実に
明日も昇る太陽以上, それは優しい
行為によって, すべての人を見渡して
一人の父の子とみなし, 父は決して
素晴らしい人間の姿を焼き尽きさせはしなかった,
幼時の葉が半ばも広がり切らぬうちは,
凄まじい人間の朽ち果てる黄金への渇望によって.

　　Poor children! on the hard world are ye cast,
A world which loves you not (save here and there
One good Samaritan), which strives to check　　　　　　40
All that is noble, all that lifts the heart
To heaven and conscious dignity. Like beasts
Ye are compelled to toil, like beasts to live,
Like beasts to die—unwept, uncomforted!
Not knowing what you are, nor whither bound
When doomed to sail, as unstarred mariners,
On that vast ocean death conducts us to.
　　　　　　　　　　　　　　　　　　　(1798)

　　哀れな子等よ!　お前らは辛い世界へ投げ出されたのだ,

お前らを愛さぬ世界（例外は時折の
40　一人のよきサマリア人だ），それは阻もうとするばかり
高貴なものすべてを，心を高めるものすべてを
天国と尊厳の自覚へと．獣のごとき
労苦をお前らは強いられ，獣のごとき生，
獣のごとき死を――悲しむ者とてなく，慰められること
もなく！
自らの何たるかを，また何処へ向かうかも知らず
止むなく船出の定め，導きの星も無き水夫のごとく，
死が我等を導くあの広大な大洋へ．

　この一節からでも分かるように，18世紀後半ようやく進展し始めた産業革命のもと，商業や交易が盛んになるにつれ，'Mammon' (1. 15) や 'Lucre's shrine' (1.27) の言葉が象徴するように，その繁栄の陰で，物質主義や拝金主義の弊害が社会全般に蔓延し，美しく平和な田舎と素朴な人間性が失われていく姿を，この詩人も見逃さなかった．開発と荒廃の今日的現象は既に18世紀の当時から存在していたわけであった．

注

1) *18th WP*, No. 219, pp. 330-1.
2) 　拙稿「ベインの愛の主題の一面―『オルーノウコウ』を中心として―(*Caliban*, No.8 加納秀夫先生還暦記念号，朝日出版社，1971年12月) 参照。
3) Ibid., No.270, pp. 416-8.
4) *New 18th V*, No.549, pp. 832-3.

XI 労働の詩

1 Stephen Duck, 'The Thresher's Labour'

18世紀英詩の見直しの動きの中で,フェミニズムの詩と並んで重要視されなければならないのは,名もなき庶民の労働の詩ではなかろうか.

その筆頭に挙げるべき詩人は,やはりスティーヴン・ダック(1705-60)であろう.南英 Wiltshire の生まれで14才までは慈善学校に通ったが,それ以後は日雇人夫として農作業のかたわら,シェイクスピアやミルトンを学んで詩作を始め,やがて宮廷で上記の詩を朗読して以来,Queen Caroline の愛顧を得て宮廷に出仕し,国王衛士に任命され,女官と再婚,30ポンドの年金と住居を下賜され,牧師となって順調な生涯かと思われたが,妻の死後の頃から憂鬱症に悩み始め,故郷を訪れての帰り Reading 近くの池に投身自殺したのであった.

出世の端緒となったこの有名な詩「脱穀夫の労働」(1730)[1]から,次の一節を読むことにしよう.

from *The Thresher's Labour*

Soon as the harvest hath laid bare the plains,

And barns well filled reward the farmer's pains,
What corn each sheaf will yield intent to hear,
And guess from thence the profits of the year,
Or else impending ruin to prevent
By paying, timely, threat'ning landlord's rent,
He calls his threshers forth: around we stand,
With deep attention waiting his command.
To each our tasks he readily divides,
10 And, pointing, to our different stations guides.
As he directs, to different barns we go;
Here two for wheat, and there for barley two.
But first, to show what he expects to find,
These words, or words like these, disclose his mind:
'So dry the corn was carried from the field,
So easily 'twill thresh, so well 'twill yield.
Sure large day's work I well may hope for now;
Come, strip, and try, let's see what you can do.'
Divested of our clothes, with flail in hand,
20 At a just distance, front to front we stand;
And first the threshall's gently swung, to prove
Whether with just exactness it will move:
That once secure, more quick we whirl them round,
From the strong planks our crabtree staves rebound,
And echoing barns return the rattling sound.
Now in the air our knotty weapons fly,
And now with equal force descend from high:

Down one, one up, so well they keep the time,
The Cyclops' hammers could not truer chime;
Nor with more heavy strokes could Etna groan, 30
When Vulcan forged the arms for Thetis' son.
In briny streams our sweat descends apace,
Drops from our locks, or trickles down our face.
No intermission in our works we know;
The noisy threshall must for ever go.
Their master absent, others safely play;
The sleeping threshall doth itself betray.
Nor yet the tedious labour to beguile,
And make the passing minutes sweetly smile,
Can we, like shepherds, tell a merry tale: 40
The voice is lost, drowned by the noisy flail.
But we may think.—Alas! what pleasing thing
Here to the mind can the dull fancy bring?
The eye beholds no pleasant object here:
No cheerful sound diverts the list'ning ear.
The shepherd well may tune his voice to sing,
Inspired by all the beauties of the spring:
No fountains murmur here, no lambkins play,
No linnets warble, and no fields look gay;
'Tis all a dull and melancholy scene, 50
Fit only to provoke the Muse's spleen.
When sooty pease we thresh, you scarce can know
Our native colour, as from work we go:

The sweat, and dust, and suffocating smoke
Make us so much like Ethiopians look,
We scare our wives, when evening brings us home,
And frighted infants think the bugbear come.
Week after week we this dull task pursue,
Unless when winnowing days produce a new,
60 A new indeed, but frequently a worse:
The threshall yields but to the master's curse.
He counts the bushels, counts how much a day,
Then swears we've idled half our time away.
'Why look ye, rogues! D'ye think that this will do?
Your neighbours thresh as much again as you.'
Now in our hands we wish our noisy tools,
To drown the hated names of rogues and fools;
But wanting those, we just like schoolboys look,
When th' angry master views the blotted book.
70 They cry their ink was faulty, and their pen;
We, 'The corn threshes bad, 'twas cut too green.'

(1730)

　　収穫のあと野の畑が裸になって,
　納屋が一杯で農夫の苦労が報われると直ぐに,
　ひと束ひと束どんな穀物が出てくるか, 聞き耳を立て,
　そこから当年の儲けを推し量る,
　あるいは差し迫る破滅を防ぐため
　脅す地主の地代を早めに払い,

XI 労働の詩

親方が脱穀夫らを呼び集めると，わしらは周りに立って，
注意深く親方の命令を待つ．
親方は各自に仕事を即座に分けて，
指さしながら，それぞれの持ち場に連れていく．   10
親方の指図のままに，わしらはそれぞれの納屋に行く．
ここは小麦に2人，あすこは大麦に2人．
だが第一に，親方は収穫の期待を示すため，
こんな言葉で次のように，心のうちをあらわに見せる．
「畑から運んだ麦はよく乾いていたぞ，
脱穀はそれだけ楽で，収穫もそれだけよいだろう：
きっと今日の仕事ははかが行く．
さあ，一肌脱いで，やってみろ，さてお前らどれだけ出
来るかな」
服を脱ぎ，殻竿を手に持って，
手頃な距離で，互いに面と向かい合い，   20
まず竿をやさしく振って，試みる
ぴったり正しく動くかどうか．
いったん決まれば，より早くわしらは竿を振り回す，
丈夫な厚板が曲がった竿を跳ね返し，
納屋にこだまして，がらがら音がまた戻る．
さて今や節くれ棒が空に飛び，
今また同じ勢いで高い空から降ってくる，
ひとつが降りれば，ひとつが上がり，それで上手に拍子
がとれて，
一つ目巨人の金槌とてもこれほど巧みに調子は合わぬ，
そしてまたエトナ山とてこれ以上重い響きで呻くまい， 30

ヴァルカンがアキレスの甲冑を作るとき,
塩辛いわしらの汗は滔々と
髪から流れ, 顔を伝って滴り落ちる.
わしらの仕事にゃ休みがなくて,
うるさい竿は動き詰め.
旦那がおらぬと, 手抜きも安全,
寝ぼける竿が論より証拠.
況してや退屈仕事を紛らせて,
快く笑って時を過ごそうなんぞできぬこと,
40　羊飼いならぬわっしらに, 陽気な話ができようか.
声は消え, うるさい竿にかき消さる.
だがしかし, わしらとても考える ―― ああ悲し! どんな
嬉しい事柄を
貧相な空想がこんな現場に運んでくれる?
ここにては楽しい物など何ひとつ目にすることがない,
気を引き立てる音なにひとつ聞き耳を立ててもありはせぬ.
羊飼いなら声整えて歌えもしよう,
春爛漫に誘われて.
ここにてはいかなる泉も囁かず, いかなる子羊も戯れぬ.
いかなるヒワも囀らず, いかなる野原も楽しげならず,
50　辺り一面, どんよりと気の滅入る風景だ,
ミューズの機嫌を損なうばかり.
黒ずんだ豆を殻竿で打つ折は, よもや知るまい
わしらの肌の色, 仕事から出て行く時は,
汗と埃と煙にむせて,
わしらはまるでエチオピア人の顔,

XI 労働の詩

女房どもはおびえきる，夕べに家へ帰る時，
幼児らはお化けが来たと怖じ気づく．
来る週も来る週もこの退屈仕事を続けるが，
籾殻を分ける日で新たな仕事があれば別，
なるほど仕事は新しい，だが大抵は尚つらい， 60
殻竿も親方の罵声にだけは降参だ．
親方は麦の重さを量っては，一日幾らと計算し，
わしらが半日怠けたと毒づいて，
「なんだお前ら，碌でなし！ これで充分と思うのか？
隣の奴らの脱穀はお前らの2倍だぞ」
さて今や，うるさい道具が手に欲しい，
悪党や阿呆の汚名を搔き消すために．
だが，そいつが無くて，わしらは餓鬼の泣きっ面，
腹を立てた先生に汚した本を睨まれて，
インクが悪い，ペンがまた，とベソをかく， 70
わっしらは「麦の脱穀まずかった，青すぎるのを刈ったから」と．

この71行の引用部分からでも推察できるように，ダックは自己の農業体験に基づいて，無為徒食の地主階級や強欲な監督のもと，脱穀という騒々しく単調な農作業を中心に，決して牧歌風にではなく，四季を通じて苛酷な労働に明け暮れる日雇人夫の厳しい生活を生々しく描いていたのである．

ただ古典的引喩や叙事詩風の比喩，詩語をちりばめて当時の教養人士の喝采を博したと思われるところは，280行を超える「脱穀夫の労働」全篇を読まなければなるまい．この詩の新鮮

な魅力と彗星のごとき詩人の名声のためか，1736年再版の詩集には，皇太子ほか5人の皇族を始めとする600人以上の予約購読者が出たほどである．[2]

ダックの後も，同じウィルトシャ州の貧農出身の女性 Ann Yearsley（1752-1806）や農民詩人 John Clare（1793-1864）たちの詩があるが，特に労働の厳しさを歌う詩は，次の時代，例えば過重な労働と低賃銀に苦しむお針子の境遇を描いたThomas Hood（1799-1845）の「シャツの唄」（'The Song of the Shirt,' 1843）などに受け継がれていくのであろう．

2　Mary Collier, 'The Woman's Labour'

次に，ダックの脱穀夫の詩に触発されたメアリ・コリア（1690?-c.1762）の詩「女性の労働」（1739）[3]を取り上げなくてはならない．副題の 'An Epistle to Mr Stephen Duck' が示すように，これはダックの詩に答えた書簡詩なのである．彼女に「女性の労働」の詩を書かせた直接の契機となったのは，例えばダックの次の2行であった．

> Ah! were their Hands so active as their Tongues,
> How nimbly then would move the Rakes and Prongs!
> 　　　　　　　　　　　　　　　　（ll.169-70）

すなわち，とかくお喋りに夢中な女労働者たちの仕事の非能率と無責任さが揶揄され，嘲けられていたのである．曰く，'prattling Females'（l.164）とか 'the tattling Croud'（l.187）と．このような女性蔑視に対し，コリアはその名誉回復のため

XI 労働の詩

に筆を執ったわけである．ダックの詩を模倣しパロディ化して反論し，ほぼパラレルに応酬するさまは，やはり「女性の労働」全篇246行に譲らざるを得ない．ここでは「プロレタリア反牧歌詩」('proletarian anti-pastoral poem')[4] としての次の一節を紹介するに止める．

from *The Woman's Labour. An Epistle to Mr Stephen Duck*

[The Washerwoman]

WHEN bright Orion glitters in the skies
In winter nights, then early we must rise;
The weather ne'er so bad, wind, rain or snow,
Our work appointed, we must rise and go,
While you on easy beds may lie and sleep,
Till light does through your chamber-windows peep.
When to the house we come where we should go,
How to get in, alas! we do not know:
The maid quite tired with work the day before,
O'ercome with sleep; we standing at the door,   10
Oppressed with cold, and often call in vain,
Ere to our work we can admittance gain.
But when from wind and weather we get in,
Briskly with courage we our work begin;
Heaps of fine linen we before us view,
Whereon to lay our strength and patience too;

Cambrics and muslins, which our ladies wear,
Laces and edgings, costly, fine and rare,
Which must be washed with utmost skill and care;
20 With holland shirts, ruffles and fringes too,
Fashions which our forefathers never knew.
For several hours here we work and slave,
Before we can one glimpse of daylight have;
We labour hard before the morning's past,
Because we fear the time runs on too fast.

　明るいオリオンの星が空にきらめくと
冬の夜でも，もうわたしらは起きねばならぬ．
風，雨，また雪と，天気がどんなに悪くても，
仕事が決まれば，起き出て行かねばならぬ，
あなた方は楽な寝床でお休みなのに，
朝の光が部屋の窓から射し込むまでは．
わたしらが行くべき家に着いたとき，
どうして入ったらよいものか，悲しいことに，分からない．
女中さんが前日の仕事ですっかり疲れ，
10 眠りこけて白河夜船．戸口に立ったわたしらは，
寒さに苦しめられて，なんど呼んでも返事がない，
そのうちやっと中に入り仕事につける．
だがしかし風雨をついて入るからは，
きびきび元気に仕事を始め，
目の前に綺麗なリンネルがうずたかい，
そこがまた辛抱と力の入れどころ，

XI 労働の詩

上質白麻,綿モスは,奥様方のお召し物,
レースや縁飾り,高価で珍しい逸品揃い,
飛び切りの腕で注意して是非洗濯をせにゃならぬ,
麻布シャツやひだ飾り,それにまた房飾り,   20
ご先祖もご存知のない流行(はやり)もの.
ここで数時間,奴隷のように働いて,
ようやく夜明けがちらと拝まれる,
必死で働く朝のうち,
時間の経つのが早過ぎる,それが気になるものだから.

  At length bright Sol illuminates the skies,
And summons drowsy mortals to arise;
Then comes our mistress to us without fail,
And in her hand, perhaps, a mug of ale
To cheer our hearts, and also to inform   30
Herself what work is done that very morn;
Lays her commands upon us, that we mind
Her linen well, nor leave the dirt behind.
Not this alone, but also to take care
We don't her cambrics nor her ruffles tear;
And these most strictly does of us require,
To save her soap and sparing be of fire;
Tells us her charge is great, nay furthermore,
Her clothes are fewer than the time before.
Now we drive on, resolved our strength to try,   40
And what we can we do most willingly;

Until with heat and work, 'tis often known,
Not only sweat but blood runs trickling down
Our wrists and fingers: still our work demands
The constant action of our labouring hands.

　とうとう輝く太陽が大空を照らし出し，
まだ眠たげな人間にさあ起きろと促せば，
その頃きまって女主人のお出ましだ，
手には，恐らく，ビールのジョッキ
30 わたしらへの景気づけ，それにまた知りたがる，
その朝どれだけ仕事ができたかと，
命令しては，気を配れ
わたしのリンネル用心と，汚れをあとに残すなと．
これで済まずに，また注意
白麻布やひだ飾り，引き裂いたりはせぬように，
こんな事をいとも厳しくお求めで，
石鹸節約，火を倹約に，
費用がかさむとお言い付け，いやそれどころかその上に，
着物の数が前より減った，とか．
40 さて今や，わたしらは馬力をかけてどんどん仕事，
出来るところは，いそいそとやる，
だが遂に暑さと仕事で，よくあることだ，
汗だけでなく，血までが滴り落ちてくる
手首や指を伝わって．それでもわたしらの仕事には
せっせと働く両手の動きが欠かせない．

XI　労働の詩　　　　　　　　　　　　　169

　Now night comes on, from whence you have relief,
But that, alas! does but increase our grief.
With heavy hearts we often view the sun,
Fearing he'll set before our work is done;
For, either in the morning or at night,　　　　　　　　50
We piece the summer's day with candlelight.
Though we all day with care our work attend,
Such is our fate, we know not when 'twill end.
When evening's come, you homeward take your way;
We, till our work is done, are forced to stay,
And, after all our toil and labour past,
Sixpence or eightpence pays us off at last;
For all our pains no prospect can we see
Attend us, but old age and poverty.

　　　　　　　　　　　　　　　　　　(1739)

　さてやがて夜が来る，あんた方には休息が，
だが悲し！　わたしらには嘆きの種が増すばかり，
心も重く，夕陽を見るたびに，
心配は，仕事が済まずに日暮れかと．
というわけは，朝のうち，あるいは夜のどちらかで，　　50
夏の日をローソクの灯で継ぎ合わす．
終日，仕事に精は出すけれど，
わたしらの運命はこんなもの，いつが終わりになるのやら．
日が暮れて，あんたらは家路へ向かっても，
わたしら仕事が終わるまで，居残りせねばなりませぬ．

骨折り仕事が済んだあと,
6ペンスか8ペンス日銭をもらって首になる.
働けど働けど, 先の見込は立たなくて
付いてくるのは, ただ老いと貧乏.

コリアもまた貧しい生まれながら, 早くから読書に親しみ, 63歳まで洗濯女を続け, 70歳頃まで農場主の家政婦を引き受けていたという. 恐らく, 田舎で労働しつつ詩作した初めてのイギリス女性として, 地主らの搾取や男性の権威に抗し, 働く女の自立意識にも目覚めたフェミニストの先覚者であったかもしれない.

3 Christopher Smart, 'A Morning-Piece, or, An Hymn for the Hay-Makers'

ダックやコリアの総じて重苦しい詩に対し, 明るい朝の楽しい労働の歌がなくもない. 『ダビデ王讃歌』(*A Song to David*, 1763) で名高い薄幸の詩人クリストファー・スマート (1722-71) の次の詩「朝の曲, あるいは乾草作りの人々への賛歌」(1748)[5] がその一例である.

A Morning-Piece, or, An Hymn for the
Hay-Makers

BRISK Chaunticleer his matins had begun,
　　And broke the silence of the night,
　　And thrice he called aloud the tardy sun,

XI 労働の詩

And thrice he hailed the dawn's ambiguous light;
Back to their graves the fear-begotten phantoms run.

元気のよい雄鶏が朝の唄を始めた,
　そして夜のしじまを破り,
　そして3度も愚図の太陽を声高に呼び,
　そして3度も暁の薄明りを喜び迎えると,
恐怖に憑かれた亡霊どもが走って墓場へ戻る.

Strong Labour got up with his pipe in his mouth,
　And stoutly strode over the dale,
He lent new perfumes to the breath of the south,
　On his back hung his wallet and flail.
Behind him came Health from her cottage of thatch,　　　10
Where never physician had lifted the latch.

逞しい労働がパイプを口に起き上がり,
谷間をのっしのっしと闊歩して,
南の風に新しい香りを送り,
頭陀袋と殻竿を背中に掛けた.
その後ろから健康が茅葺きの家からやって来た,　　　10
医者なんぞその家のかんぬきを外したことがない.

First of the village Colin was awake,
And thus he sung, reclining on his rake:
　Now the rural graces three

    Dance beneath yon maple tree;
    First the vestal Virtue, known
    By her adamantine zone;
    Next to her in rosy pride;
    Sweet Society, the bride;
20   Last Honesty, full seemly dressed
    In her cleanly home-spun vest.
The abbey bells in wak'ning rounds
    The warning peal have giv'n;
And pious Gratitude resounds
    Her morning hymn to heav'n.

村一番にコリンが目覚め,
熊手にもたれて,歌うには,
    いま田舎の3女神
    向こうの楓(かえで)の木の下で踊る,
    まず純潔のウェスタの操,名の知れた
    堅牢無比の帯を持ち,
    隣りにはバラ色の誇りに輝いて
    快い仲間の花嫁が,
20   最後に正直が,嗜みのよい服をつけ
    きれいな手紡ぎチョッキに包まれて.
寺の鐘が目覚ましに繰り返し
    戒めのごとく鳴り渡る.
そして敬虔な感謝の念がとどろかす
    朝の賛歌を天上へ.

XI 労働の詩　　　　　　　　　　　　　173

All nature wakes—the birds unlock their throats,
And mock the shepherd's rustic notes.
　All alive o'er the lawn,
　Full glad of the dawn,
　　The little lambkins play,　　　　　　　　　　30
Sylvia and Sol arise,—and all is day—

自然がすべて目を覚ます―鳥たちは喉をゆるめて,
羊飼いの素朴な調べの真似をする.
　芝地でほんとに生き生きと,
　夜明けがとても嬉しくて,
　　小さな子羊たちが戯れる,　　　　　　　　　　30
シルヴィアと太陽が身を起こし,――世はすべて朝になる――

　Come, my mates, let us work,
　And all hands to the fork,
While the sun shines, our hay-cocks to make,
　So fine is the day,
　And so fragrant the hay,
That the meadow's as blithe as the wake.

　さあ来たれ, わが仲間たち, ともに働こう,
　全員熊手だ,
日の照るうちに, 干し草の山作り,
　天気は上々,
　干し草は香りがよくて,

牧場は祭りのように楽しげだ.

>   Our voices let's raise
>   In Phoebus's praise;
> 40 Inspired by so glorious a theme,
>   Our musical words
>   Shall be joined by the birds,
>   And we'll dance to the tune of the stream.

(1748)

われらは声を張り上げて
太陽神を言祝ごう.
40 かくも見事な主題に励まされ,
歌の言葉に
鳥たちを加わらせ,
せせらぎの音に合わせて踊るのだ.

　スマートには農事詩 'The Hop-Garden'（1752）もあるが, これは農作業の実写ではなかろう. 一目瞭然, 抽象名詞の擬人化の羅列がそれを教える. この朝の歌の明るさは, 飲酒癖で借財を重ね, 精神異常を来たし, 入獄中に死亡した人間のものとは思われぬほどである. 村の若者 Colin や村娘 Sylvia, 羊飼い, 鳥, 子羊, 牧場, 太陽神と古典的な田園牧歌風景に付き物の道見立てが並び, これは写実に徹した厳しい労働歌とは対照的であろう.

　このほか, ジャコバイトで賛美歌も書いた詩人 John Byrom

(1692-1763) の「満足, あるいは幸せな職人の唄」(Contentment, or The Happy Workman's Song, 1773)[6] のように, 貧しくても何ひとつ不足をかこつことなく, 政争を離れて, 神の御旨のままに満足して生きる田舎職人を歌ったものもある. しかし, これはもはや牧歌や農耕歌というよりは, むしろ既に先述した「隠退の神話」の流れに繋がるものであろう.

注

1) *New 18th V*, No.156, pp.224-5. この労働の詩については, 続いて取り上げる Mary Collier の 'The Woman's Labour' とともに Duck-Collier 論争をなすもので, 次の拙稿を参照にして頂ければ幸いである.「Stephen Duck と Mary Collier —— 脱穀夫と洗濯女の歌」(「日本ジョンソン協会年報」No.23, 1999 年 5 月, pp.17-22.) Cf. John Goodridge, *Rural Life in Eighteenth-Century English Poetry* (Cambridge University Press, 1995). 特に, Thomson, Duck, Collier を論じた次の第一部が参考になろう. 'Part I "Hard labour we most chearfully pursue': three poets on rural work, pp.11-88.

なお, Duck の詩のテキストは *The Augustan Reprint Society*, No.230 (University of California, 1985) では 1736 年の再版 (286 行) を採り, *Eighteenth-Century Poetry: The Annotated Anthology*, ed. by David Fairer and Christine Gerrard (Blackwell Publishers Ltd., 1999) では 1730 年の初版 (283 行) を採っている.

2) 上記の *The Augustan Reprint Society*, No.230 (pp.xxi-xxxi) に予約講読者のリストが A, B, C 順に付せられている.

3) *18th WP*, No.113, pp.172-3. Anna Laetitia Barbauld (1743-

1825) にも 'Washing-Day' (1797) と題する詩がある. Cf. *18th WP*, No.202, pp.308-10.
4)　John Goodridge, p.6. なお, コリアのダックに対する「ほぼパラレルな応酬」については, 注1の拙稿において, その幾つかの具体例を指摘した.
5)　*New 18th V*, No.283, pp.427-8.
6)　*18th V*, No.148, pp.230-1.

XII 貧窮の詩

1 Mary Barber, 'On seeing an Officer's Widow distracted, . . .'

　石川啄木ではないが,「はたらけど　はたらけど猶わが生活楽にならざり　ぢっと手を見る」というような貧困と孤独を歌う詩に移ってみよう.

　まずアイルランドはダブリンの羊毛服地仕立屋の妻メアリ・バーバ (c.1690-1757), 夫の店を手伝いながら, 主に子供の教育のために詩作したという. 時のアイルランド総督であった Lord Carteret に, ある陸軍士官未亡人の窮状を詩で訴えたことがあり, Swift がパトロン役を買って出て, しばしば彼女を援助したものである.

　「さる士官の未亡人の狂えるを見て, 寡婦年金の遅れのため, 長期間にわたる懇願も空しく絶望に追いやられて」(1734)[1] と題する次の 32 行を紹介しよう.

On seeing an Officer's Widow distracted, who had
been driven to Despair by a long and fruitless
Solicitation for the Arrears of her Pension

O WRETCH! hath madness cured thy dire despair?
Yes—All thy sorrows now are light as air:
No more you mourn your once loved husband's fate,
Who bravely perished for a thankless state.
For rolling years thy piety prevailed;
At length, quite sunk—thy hope, thy patience failed.
Distracted now you tread on life's last stage,
Nor feel the weight of poverty and age:
How blest in this, compared with those whose lot
10 Dooms them to miseries, by you forgot!

 おお哀れな人よ！ 狂気があなたの恐ろしい絶望を癒しているのか？
そうです ―― あなたの悲しみは今すべて空気のように軽い．
もはやあなたはかつての愛する夫の運命を歎くことはない，
夫は勇敢に恩知らずの国のために戦死したのだ．
めぐる幾年間か，あなたは敬虔な気持ちで一杯だった，
だが遂に，すっかり落ちぶれて ―― あなたの希望，あなたの忍耐はくずおれた．
気が狂った今あなたは人生最後の時期に来て，
貧しさや老いの重荷も感じない．
これは何と幸せなことか，あの運命の
10 悲惨な人々に比べて，あなたはそれを忘れた！

XII 貧窮の詩

  Now, wild as winds, you from your offspring fly,
Or fright them from you with distracted eye;
Rove through the streets; or sing, devoid of care,
With tattered garments and dishevelled hair;
By hooting boys to higher frenzy fired,
At length you sink, by cruel treatment tired,
Sink into sleep, an emblem of the dead,
A stone thy pillow, the cold earth thy bed.

 さて今や,風のように奔放に,あなたは子供たちから飛んでいく,
かと思えば狂おしい目でかれらを脅やかす,
街をさまよい,あるいは歌う,何の煩うこともなく,
よれよれの服と振り乱した髪で.
嘲ける坊主らに煽られてますます狂乱し,
遂にあなたは倒れ込む,むごい仕打ちに疲れ果て,
眠りへと沈みこむ,死者の標章,
石を枕に,冷たい土地を床にして.

  O tell it not; let none the story hear,
Lest Britain's martial sons should learn to fear:
And when they next the hostile wall attack,
Feel the heart fail, the lifted arm grow slack;
And pausing cry—'Though death we scorn to dread,
Our orphan offspring, must they pine for bread?
See their loved mothers into prisons thrown,

And, unrelieved, in iron bondage groan?'

　　おお，それを語るな，その話は誰にも聞かせるな，
20　イギリスの勇ましい息子らが恐怖を覚えることのないように．
　この次にかれらが敵の城壁を攻めるとき，
　心が萎えて，振り上げた腕がだらりと緩み，
　立ち止まって叫ぶことのないように——「われらは死を怖れはせぬが，
　孤児となった子供らが，パンを求めて寰れはせぬか?
　いとしい母親が牢に投げ込まれ，
　救いの手もなく，鉄の鎖に呻くのを見なければならぬのではないか?」

　　Britain, for this impending ruin dread;
　Their woes call loud for vengeance on thy head:
　Nor wonder, if disasters wait your fleets;
30　Nor wonder at complainings in your streets.
　Be timely wise; arrest th' uplifted hand,
　Ere pestilence or famine sweep the land.

(1734)

　　イギリスよ，この差し迫る破滅を恐れよ，
　かれらの悲しみが汝の頭上に復讐を声高く叫ぶ．
　また不思議はない，災厄が汝の艦隊を待ち受けようと，
30　また不思議はない，汝の街にあふれる不平不満も．

速やかに悟れ，持ち上げられた手を止めよ，
疫病や飢餓が国中を襲わぬうちに．

　このように，国のため命を捧げた軍人の未亡人が，何の補償も受けられず，遂に路頭に迷い，精神錯乱に陥る状況を描き，その冷酷な政治の無策に悲憤慷慨やる方ない女性の詩であった．

2　Thomas Moss, 'The Beggar'

　次はトマス・モス（1740?-1808）による文字どおりの貧窮の詩「乞食」（1769）[2]をみよう．賛美歌調の押韻で，11連44行の詩である．

The Beggar

P<small>ITY</small> the sorrows of a poor old man!
Whose trembling limbs have borne him to your door,
Whose days are dwindled to the shortest span.
Oh! give relief—and heaven will bless your store.

These tattered clothes my poverty bespeak,
These hoary locks proclaim my lengthened years,
And many a furrow in my grief-worn cheek
Has been a channel to a stream of tears.

Yon house, erected on the rising ground,
With tempting aspect drew me from my road,

10

For Plenty there a residence has found,
And Grandeur a magnificent abode.

    Hard is the fate of the infirm and poor!
Here craving for a morsel of their bread,
A pampered menial forced me from the door
To seek a shelter in a humbler shed.

    Oh! take me to your hospitable dome,
Keen blows the wind and piercing is the cold!
Short is my passage to the friendly tomb,
For I am poor—and miserably old.

    貧しい老人の悲しみを哀れんでくれ!
震える手足であんたの戸口までやって来た,
わしの命はいま旦夕(たんせき)に迫る.
おお! 救いの手を —— そうすれば天はあんたの蔵を祝福されよう.

    このぼろぼろの服はわしの貧乏の生きじるし,
この白髪はわしの長びいた歳月の証明だ,
悲しみに褻れた頬に幾多の皺が
涙の小川の水路となった.

    向こうの家が, 小高い丘に立ち,
誘うような様子で, わしを道から引きつけた,

豊かさがそこに住まいを見つけ，
壮麗が豪華な邸を見つけていたから．

　体の弱った貧しい者の運命は辛いもの！
ここでパンを一切れ所望をすると，
増長した下郎が戸口から追い立てた
ひどいあばら屋にでも住処を探せと．

　おお！ わしをあんたの温かい館へ連れて行っておくれ，
吹く風は身を切り，寒さは肌を刺す！
やさしい墓への旅もあと僅か，
わしは貧しくて──惨めな老人なのだ． 20

Should I reveal the source of every grief,
If soft humanity e'er touched your breast,
Your hands would not withhold the kind relief,
And tears of pity could not be repressed.

Heaven sends misfortunes — why should we repine?
'Tis heaven has brought me to that state you see:
And your condition may be soon like mine,
The child of sorrow and of misery.

　もしわしが嘆きのもとをみな漏らし，
優しい人情があんたの胸に触れたなら，

あんたとて親切な救いの手を控えはすまい，
同情の涙がとても抑えられはせんだろう．

　天が不運を送るのだ —— どうして不平を言えようか？
わしのご覧の有様はみな天のなさること，
やがてあんたのご身分もわしと同じになるのかも，
悲しみとそして惨めな境遇に．

　A little farm was my paternal lot,
30　Then like the lark I sprightly hailed the morn;
　But ah! oppression forced me from my cot,
　My cattle died and blighted was my corn.

　My daughter—once the comfort of my age!
　Lured by a villain from her native home,
　Is cast abandoned on the world's wide stage,
　And doomed in scanty poverty to roam.

　My tender wife—sweet soother of my care!
　Struck with sad anguish at the stern decree,
　Fell, lingering fell, a victim to despair,
40　And left the world to wretchedness and me.

　Pity the sorrows of a poor old man!
　Whose trembling limbs have borne him to your door,
　Whose days are dwindled to the shortest span.

XII 貧窮の詩　　　　　　　　185

Oh! give relief—and heaven will bless your store.
(1769)

　小さな農場が父親譲りの土地だった，
その頃は雲雀(ひばり)のように元気よく朝を迎えたものだった．　　　30
しかし，ああ！　圧制がわしを田舎屋から追い立てた，
牛は死に，そして小麦は枯れはてた．

　わしの娘は —— かつては老いの杖柱！
悪党にかどわかされて家を出て，
広い世間に打ち棄てられて，
いま極貧に放浪するが身の定め．

　いとしい妻は —— わしの苦労の宥め役！
厳しい定めに苦悩のあまり，
倒れこみ，長患いの果て，絶望の犠牲となって，
この世には惨めさとわしだけが残された．　　　40

　貧しい老人の悲しみを哀れんでくれ！
震える手足であんたの戸口までやって来た，
わしの命はいま旦夕に迫る．
おお！　救いの手を —— そうすれば天はあんたの蔵を祝
福されよう．

このように，一人の老農夫が，圧制に苦しめられ，次第に農
耕もままならず，娘は行方知れず，妻は絶望の死，遂に流浪の

乞食となった貧乏物語である. 一見バラッド風な素朴な訴えによって, かえって社会や政治の悪を浮き彫りにしていよう.

3 Anonymous, 'Between an Unemployed Artist and his Wife'

最後に, もう一つ読み人知らずの作「失業中の職人とその妻の間で」(1775)[3] と題する夫婦の対話形式の詩 166 行を紹介して, 貧窮の詩を締め括ることにする.

ANONYMOUS
Between an Unemployed Artist and his Wife

[Alone

She HARD is my fate, thus to want bread;
Curse on the day that I did wed!
While single I had food to eat,
My labour still procured me meat;
In a good place I lived at ease,
No careful thoughts my mind to tease;
In peace enjoyed a plenteous board,
With even delicacies stored;
Till simple love, and mounting pride,
10 First drew my foolish thoughts aside;
Soothed my fond ears with flatt'ry's sound,
And whispered pleasures should abound;
Service I learned thus to detest,

A place was irksome to my breast,
Thoughts of dependence broke my rest.
A master soon became my dread—
I cried, 'I'll work no more for bread;
I'll mistress of my actions move,
United to the man I love'.
I longed to taste a marriage life, 20
So plunged into a sea of strife;
And thinking to become more free,
Gave up at once my liberty,
To thraldom and neccessity;
Consented to accept a chain,
And let two tyrants o'er me reign—
Want and a husband, who still rule,
Confining me now passion's cool;
Distresses will affection damp,
Gold is the oil that feeds love's lamp. 30
Here horrors darken all the place,
There famine stares me in the face;
For bread my children loudly cry,
Which I am forced—forced to deny.

      [*Enter Husband.*

You're come—What, have you met success?
With aught will heav'n our wishes bless,
To mitigate our sharp distress?

〔独りで

妻　わたしの運命はつらい，こんなにパンがないなんて，
　　結婚した日など呪われておしまい！
　　独身の間は食べ物があった，
　　わたしの働きでいつも食事ができて，
　　立派なお邸で楽に暮らせた，
　　心を悩ます心配事もなく，
　　のどかに豊かな食卓を楽しんだ，
　　珍しいご馳走までいろいろあって．
　　でもとうとう無邪気な愛と募る誇りが
10　まずわたしの愚かな考えをわきに呼び，
　　お世辞たらたらわたしの浅はかな耳をくすぐって，
　　楽しいことが一杯になると囁いた．
　　こうして奉公勤めが厭になり，
　　屋敷が内心うんざりで，
　　下女と思うと気が休まらず，
　　そのうち主人が不安の種になり——
　　叫んで言った，「パンのためにはもう働きません，
　　自分のことは自分でします，
　　愛する人と一緒になって」
20　わたしは結婚生活を味わいたくて，
　　限りない奮闘の海に飛び込んだ．
　　もっと自由になると予期したが，
　　すぐに自由をあきらめて，
　　奴隷と貧乏の身になった．
　　鎖を付けるのに同意して，

XII 貧窮の詩　　　　　　　　　　　　189

暴君2人がわたしを支配——
困窮と亭主とが，いつも君臨，
熱が冷めてもまだ縛られて，
難儀が情けを湿らせて，
お金が愛の灯をともす油というわけで.　　　　　　　30
こうなるとぞっとするほど恐ろしく家中が暗くなり，
飢えがわたしを睨みつけ，
子供らはパンを求めて泣き叫ぶ，
そんなこと，どうしてもどうしても認めるわけにはいきません.

〔夫が登場.

お帰りなさい——なにか，首尾よくいきました?
何か神様がわたしらの望みを叶えて下さるの,
わたしらの身を切るような苦しみを和らげようと?

He 　No; there's no diff'rence in our fate—
　　　Famine does but procrastinate
　　　That death which quickly must attend,　　　40
　　　And in the grave my mis'ries end:
　　　I come home empty as I went,
　　　Only more tired, and less content.
She 　Is there no work then to be got?
He 　Not the least job—indeed there's not:
　　　The masters say their shops are full,
　　　And business either dead or dull;
　　　'They've goods enough' is all their cry,

     And yet no customers to buy;
50   Their correspondents daily break—
     Their all's continually at stake;
     Scarce any money circulates,
     But paper due at distant dates;
     Their debts are large, and they must stay,
     For all are tardy now in pay:
     Respecting debts, both great and small,
     Happy to get them in at all;
     Many as desp'rate are confessed,
     And dubious e'en the very best.

夫　　いや，わしらの運に変わりはない──
　　　飢えがただ延ばすだけ
40　　足早に付いてくるあの死をな，
　　　墓に入ればわしの不幸も終わる，
　　　行きも帰りも手ぶらだが，
　　　草臥(くたび)れもうけで，ますます不満．
妻　　じゃ仕事は何にももらえないの？
夫　　仕事はからきし無い──ほんとに無い．
　　　親方らが言うことにゃ，店は一杯
　　　商売ほとんど上がったり，
　　　「品物は充分あるんだが」と異口同音，
　　　だが買うてくれる客がない．
50　　取引先が日々つぶれ──
　　　持ち物がみな次々賭けられて，

金がほとんど回らない,
先きで支払う手形だけ,
かれらの借金は莫大で, きっと残るにちがいない,
すべての払いがいま遅れ,
借金は, 大小いずれでも
取り立てられれば幸いで,
多くは見込みがないとくる,
一番良いのでも危ないもんだ.

She   Ah! I believe my heart will break.   60
He   You must these ills with patience take.
She   Preach the sea calm, when the winds rage;
Can patience hungry mouths assuage?
Will patience gives your babes a meal,
Who all the pangs of famine feel?
For bread to me all day they cry,
While I cannot their wants supply,
Till through fatigue they fall asleep,
Then wake again to call and weep.
Will patience make your children still,   70
Or their poor empty bellies fill?
Our landlord, ask if he's content
Your patience to receive for rent;
The baker's bill will patience pay,
Or send the butcher pleased away?
While you are out in seeking work,

They join to use me like a Turk;
With threats and menaces pursue,
Of what they say they're bent to do;
80   In vain to them were patience thrown,
For frequently I lose my own.

60 妻 ああ！ほんとに胸が張り裂けそう．
    夫 この災難は辛抱せにゃならん．
    妻 海に静まれとお説教，暴風が吹き荒れている時に，
        辛抱したら飢えた口が満たされますか？
        辛抱したら幼児らに食事が出てくるの，
        飢えの苦しみが身にしみている幼児らに？
        一日中パンが欲しいと泣くのです，
        子供の願いを叶えてやれず，
        とうとう子供ら疲れて眠り込む，
        また目を覚ましては泣き叫ぶ．
70   辛抱であんたの子等が静まりますか，
        ひもじいお腹(なか)が一杯になるの？
        地主にも不足がないか訊いとくれ
        辛抱を地代のかわりに納めても．
        辛抱でパン屋のつけが払えるの，
        肉屋を笑顔で帰せるの？
        あんたが仕事を探しに出た間，
        二人の扱い，わたしをまるでトルコ人，
        脅迫，威嚇で悩ませ続け，
        言う事は必ずやるぞ，と御口上．

XII 貧窮の詩

辛抱もあの人たちにゃ効き目がなくて, 80
わたしの方が何回も堪忍袋の緒が切れる.

He   Alas! what would you have me do?
She Can't you some other trade pursue?
　　　 Perhaps you might some work obtain,
　　　 T' enable us to live again.
He   'Tis all the same—all trades are dead;
　　　 Through town a gen'ral murmur's spread:
　　　 Besides, to take a trade in hand
　　　 I do not clearly understand—
　　　 Masters would call me stupid sot, 90
　　　 And say they've better workmen got;
　　　 'Think you,' they'd say, 'that we'll employ
　　　 A man our business to destroy?
　　　 Trade of itself is very lame;
　　　 You'd bring our shop at once to shame,
　　　 And hurt our credit and our name.
　　　 No, while good hands can be procured,
　　　 Bunglers ought not to be endured.'
　　　 Such, such would be the master's song,
　　　 While thus the men would use their tongue: 100
　　　 'Business is not already bad,
　　　 Though there's scarce any to be had,
　　　 But you an interloper come
　　　 Where all is full, and there's no room.

Too indolent you seem to be,

For such still love variety;

And like a lounging lazy drone,

You steal our trade and quit your own.'

Thus neither good success nor gains

110 Would recompense my honest pains.

夫　あーあ！　わしにどうして欲しいのだ？
妻　何かほかの仕事がやれないの？
　　そうすりゃ多少は仕事にありつけて，
　　もう一度まともに暮らせるわ．
夫　みんな同じよ——商売はみんな上がったり，
　　町中に不平不満が一杯だ，
　　今さら商売を始めるなんぞ
　　とんとわしには分からねえ——
90　親方らわしを大馬鹿者と罵って，
　　もっとはましな職人がいると言うだろう．
　　「お前な」，親方らは言うだろう，「わしらが雇うと思うのか
　　仕事を潰すような男をな？
　　商売自体が左前，
　　お前なら直ぐに店の恥さらし，
　　信用も名前も台なしだ．
　　そうなんだ，よい職人が手に入る限り，
　　無器用者など我慢ならねえ」
　　そんな，そんなところが親方の歌い文句よ，

XII 貧窮の詩　　　　　　　　　　195

職人たちの言い草はまあざっとこんな風,　　　　　　　100
「景気はもう悪くない,
手に入る仕事はほとんどないが,
お前が邪魔にやって来る
どこも手が足りて, 空きなど全然ないところに.
お前はどうやら怠け者,
そういう手合いは移り気で,
のらくら雄蜂(おんな)と同じで,
こちらの商売を盗んでは, 自分の商売を止めにする」
こうなると成功も儲けもふいになり,
まともな苦労は報われん.　　　　　　　　　　　　110

She　What can we do?—Have you no friends
　　　For fortune's frowns to make amends?
　　　None that, in this our scene of woe,
　　　A little succour would bestow?

He　I've tried them all a thousand ways;
　　　All those who, in more prosp'rous days,
　　　The firmest friendship to me swore,
　　　And learned their bounty to implore;
　　　But all in vain, their *words* were wind,
　　　And, oh! their *deeds*—unkind, unkind.　　　　　120
　　　It pains, it tortures me to speak
　　　The cruelty I've met this week;
　　　While I had money, I had friends,
　　　Who meant to serve their private ends;

The friendship of these grov'ling men
Was to my circumstances then;
Now in the world no friendship reigns;
'Tis marred with interested stains;
And those who think this passion true,
130 An airy phantom but pursue;
Which when they vainly think they've caught,
Will 'scape them quick as nimble thought.
Of friendship judge by my success
In this our imminent distress:
The first whose heart I thought to touch
Was one who often promised much;
But he cried out with careless air,
'You're idle, that's the whole affair;
Do not on my good nature press;
140 I can't encourage idleness.'
Another, fond of hoarded pelf,
Replied, 'Indeed I'm poor myself.'
One said, 'You joke—you don't speak true,
I'm sure there's work enough to do;
Then learn to turn yourself about,
And seek some snug employment out;
Fortune will kindly for you carve:
While you have hands you cannot starve.'
Another cried, 'Why, go to sea,
150 You'll make yourself and family;

XII 貧窮の詩

```
            The sea you know will not refuse;
            A better thing you cannot choose.'
            This asks me if I thought him mad,
            To lend where matters were so bad;
            And that was quite amazed to find
            That he should come across my mind.
            Thus all in diff'rent ways denied,
            And bid me for myself provide;
            And tried to hide ingratitude,
            Beneath advice or sayings shrewd.              160
She    Then at the last, what hope remains,
            To end or mitigate our pains?
He     There's one dull light to cheer our gloom;
            A workhouse is our certain doom.
            Thither we all, alas! must go,
            Where death will quickly end my woe.
```

(1775)

妻　　わたしらどうしましょう?——友達があんたにないかしら
　　不景気づらを埋め合わせてくれるような?
　　誰ひとり，このわたしらの窮状に
　　ちょっと助けてくれる人がないかしら?
夫　　いろいろみんなに当たってみたが,
　　あの連中，もっと景気のよい折は,
　　まことに固い友情をわしに誓ってくれたもの,
　　そこで彼等の情けを頼ってみたが,

すっかり駄目で，奴等の言葉は風だった，
120　そしてああ！　奴等の行為は――不人情，不人情．
　　　心が痛み，苦しい想いで話をするが
　　　今週ひどい仕打ちを受けたのだ．
　　　金があるときゃ，味方があった，
　　　みな己の役に立てようとの腹づもり．
　　　こんな卑劣な奴等の友情は
　　　あの頃のわしの境遇のため，
　　　今の世じゃ友情なんぞはやらない，
　　　利欲の染みで汚されている，
　　　この情熱を真実のものとみる人は
130　空しい幻影を追うだけのこと．
　　　自慢げにやれ捕まえたと思っても，
　　　はしこい想いと同じでするりと抜ける．
　　　友情はわしの結果で考えろ，
　　　このわしらの差し迫った窮境で．
　　　まず最初，情けに訴えてみようとした奴は
　　　よく山ほどの約束をした男，
　　　だがしかし，彼奴が無頓着な素振りでわめくには，
　　　「お前は怠け者，それがすべての原因だ，
　　　わしの人のよさにつけこむな，
140　怠惰の奨励はできかねる」
　　　もう一人，不浄の蓄財が好きな奴，
　　　こう答えやがった，「実はわしも貧乏だ」
　　　一人が言った，「お前冗談を――お前嘘だろう，
　　　やる仕事はきっと十分あるもんだ．

XII 貧窮の詩

だから方向転換をやってみて，
なにか楽な仕事を捜し出せ，
運勢がやさしく道を開いてくれる，
手がある限り飢えはせん」
また一人が大声出した，「なあ，船乗りになれ，
身も立ち家族も養える，
海なら厭とは言うまいぜ，
これよりましなことはない」
前の男が訊いてくる，気違いとでも思うのか，
左前のお前に貸すなんて．
後の男はびっくり仰天，
わしの頭に浮かぶとは，と．
こうして皆がそれぞれに断わった，
自分でなにか工面せよ，と．
そうして恩知らずを隠そうとした，
助言とか抜け目ない言い草の陰に隠れて．

妻　それなら結局，どんな望みが残っているの，
　　わたしらの苦労が終わるとか和らぐために？
夫　わしらの闇に射す鈍い光がひとつある，
　　救貧院がわしらの確かな運命だ．
　　そこへ皆，悲しいことだが，行かねばならん，
　　そこで死ねばわしの悩みも直ぐ終わる．

　何と哀れな夫婦の貧窮問答であろう．いつの世にも，とりわけ産業革命の幕開けの時代には，日の当たらぬ片隅で，このような生活を送らざるを得ぬ人々が少なくなかったと思われる．

苦い人情の機微をついた貧乏物語ではある.

注

1) *18th WP*, No.89, pp.126-7.
2) *New 18th V*, No.357, pp.552-3.
3) Ibid., No.402, pp.630-3. 64行目の gives (*sic*).

XIII 愛国歌

1 Henry Fielding, 'THe Roast Beef of Old England'

イギリス人が自分の生まれた英国を称賛したとしても，それはさして不思議なことではない．例えば，シェイクスピアの場合，『リチャード2世』(II.i.40-68) のなかで，John of Gaunt が身近に迫る死を前にして，現状を憂うる余り国を愛する悲痛な言葉を残した．その有名な数行を引用しておこう．

> This royal throne of kings, this scepter'd isle,
> This earth of majesty, this seat of Mars,
> This other Eden, demi-paradise,
> This fortress built by Nature for herself
> Against infection and the hand of war,
> This happy breed of men, this little world,
> This precious stone set in the silver sea,
>   ⋮   (II.i.40-46)

また英仏の百年戦争を制した明君を描いた『ヘンリー5世』にしても，イギリス萬歳の歴史劇にほかならず，今なおイギリス国民の愛国心を喚起するものであろう．

18世紀の愛国歌は偉大な小説家の一人フィールディング (1707-54) の「古き英国のローストビーフ」(1731; 1733)[1] から始めよう.

The Roast Beef of Old England

WHEN mighty rost Beef was the *Englishman*'s Food,
　　It enobled our Hearts, and enriched our Blood;
Our Soldiers were brave, and our Courtiers were good.
　　Oh the Rost Beef of Old *England,*
　　And Old *Enlgand*'s Rost Beef!

Then, *Britons,* from all nice Dainties refrain,
Which effeminate *Italy, France,* and *Spain*;
And mighty Rost Beef shall command on the Main.
　　Oh the Rost Beef, &c.
The Grub-Street Opera, 1731; *Don Quixote in England,* 1733

でっかい焼肉をイギリス男が食ってた頃は,
われらの心は気高くなって, われらの生き血は豊かになった.
われらの兵士は勇敢で, われらの公家衆みな立派.
おお古き英国のローストビーフ,
古き英国の焼肉よ!

だから，ブリトン人たちよ，凝った珍味は食べるでないぞ，
イタリア，フランス，スペインとそいつが女々しくやわにする，
でっかい焼肉こそが四海を知ろしめす．
　おお古き英国のローストビーフ
　古き英国の焼肉よ！

　この威勢のよい唄は Hogarth の版画「カレーの門」(*Calais Gate*, 1748/49) を想い出させる．カレーの門近く，痩せこけて飢餓に苦しむフランス兵が，運び込まれるイギリスの大きなローストビーフの肉塊をいかにも羨ましげに眺め，そばで肥えたフランス人修道士が早速に指で味見をしようとしている例の風刺画である．屈強なブリトン人魂を養う源は，イギリスの代表料理ローストビーフにあり，というわけで，フィールディングはホガースと並んで観客の愛国心を掻き立てたにちがいない．

　続いて，Richard Leveridge (1670-1758) にも，フィールディングの「ローストビーフ」賛歌の第1連と2行のリフレインをそっくりそのまま取り入れて全7連にした唄 'A Song in Praise of Old English Roast Beef' (1735)[2] があった．やはりフランスとスペインを敵に見立てての愛国心を謳歌したものである．だが，もはやこの唄を掲げ試訳を添えるには及ぶまい．

　2　James Thomson, 'Rule Britannia'
次はスコットランド出身の詩人，『四季』(*The Seasons*,

1730) で名高いトムソン (1700-48) の「非公式の国歌」('the unofficial national anthem')[3] とも称される国民歌を取り上げたい. 友人 Mallet と合作の仮面劇 *Alfred* (1740) の中で発表されたものである.[4]

Rule Britannia

WHEN *Britain* first, at heaven's command,
 Arose from out the azure main;
This was the charter of the land,
 And guardian Angels sung *this* strain:
  'Rule, *Britannia,* rule the waves;
  '*Britons* never will be slaves.'

まずブリテンが, 天の命令で,
紺碧の海から生まれたときに,
これがこの国の憲章となって,
守護天使たちがこの歌を歌った.
「支配せよ, ブリタニア, 四海の波を支配せよ,
 ブリトン人は決して奴隷にはならぬ」

The nations, not so blest as thee,
 Must, in their turns, to tyrants fall:
While thou shalt flourish great and free,
 The dread and envy of them all.
  'Rule, &c.

XIII 愛国歌　　　　　　　　　　　　　205

諸々の国は，汝ほどには恵まれず，
次々に，暴君たちに屈伏せずにはおられない．
だが汝は偉大にして自由に栄え，
世界の脅威と羨望の的とならん．
　「支配せよ，…」

Still more majestic shalt thou rise,
　　More dreadful, from each foreign stroke:
As the loud blast that tears the skies,
　　Serves but to root thy native oak.
　　　'Rule, &c.

いやましに堂々と汝は立ち上がる，
外敵の襲来のたび，脅威を増して．
空をつんざく騒々しい突風が，
汝の地に生まれた樫の根を固めるだけのように．
　「支配せよ，…」

Thee haughty tyrants ne'er shall tame:
　　All their attempts to bend thee down,
Will but arrouse thy generous flame;
　　But work their woe, and thy renown.
　　　'Rule, &c.

汝ばかりは威丈高な暴君らも手なづけはせぬ．
汝を屈伏せんとする試みはすべて，

汝の高潔な怒りの焔を搔き立て,
みずからを苦しめ,汝の名を挙げるのみ.
「支配せよ,…」

To thee belongs the rural reign;
　Thy cities shall with commerce shine;
All thine shall be the subject main,
　And every shore it circles thine.
　　　'Rule, &c.

田園の統治は汝のもの,
汝の都市は交易で輝き,
海も汝に臣下の礼をとり,
津々浦々に汝を囲む.
「支配せよ,…」

The Muses, still with freedom found,
　Shall to thy happy coast repair:
Blest isle! with matchless beauty crown'd,
　And manly hearts to guard the fair.
　　　'Rule, *Britannia,* rule the waves:
　　　'*Britons* never will be slaves.'

Alfred: A Masque, Act ii, 1740

詩神らは,常に自由と共にあり,
汝の幸せな岸辺に赴くであろう.

XIII 愛国歌　　　　　　　　　　207

　幸多い小島よ！　比類ない美しさで飾られ,
　雄々しい心がその美しきものを守る.
　「支配せよ, ブリタニア, 四海の波を支配せよ,
　　ブリトン人は決して奴隷にはならぬ」

　また, William Cowper (1731-1800) にも, このトムソンと同工異曲のイギリス賛歌がある. 『務め』(*The Task,* 1785) の第2巻の中から有名な詩行を掲げておこう.[5]

Slaves cannot breathe in England

SLAVES cannot breathe in England; if their lungs
Receive our air, that moment they are free;
They touch our country, and their shackles fall.
(ll.40-2)

England

ENGLAND, with all thy faults, I love thee still—
My country! and, while yet a nook is left
Where English minds and manners may be found,
Shall be constrain'd to love thee. Though thy clime
Be fickle, and thy year most part deform'd
With dripping rains, or wither'd by a frost,
I would not yet exchange thy sullen skies,
And fields without a flow'r, for warmer France

With all her vines; nor for Ausonia's groves
Of golden fruitage, and her myrtle bow'rs.　　(ll.206-15)

　これに続いてクーパーは，国威を世界に発揚した雄弁な政治家 Chatham こと the Elder Pitt や，Quebec でフランス軍を撃破した James Wolfe 将軍の後に続く者出でよ，と熱烈な祖国愛を披瀝していたものである．

3　Tobias Smollett, 'The Tears of Scotland. Written in the Year 1746'

　スコットランド出身の小説家スモレット（1721-71）の場合は，愛国心というよりも愛郷心，郷土愛ということになろうか．「スコットランドの涙，1746年作」(1746)[6] を読めば，そのことは明白である．

　その執筆年から分かるように，この詩は1715年に次ぐ再度の「ジャコバイト反乱」('Jacobite Rebellion') の終息を哀悼したものである．言うまでもなく，ジャコバイト運動は名誉革命後の Hanover 王朝に対し，正統ともいうべき Stuart 王家の王位回復を目指した運動であってみれば，これは決して「反乱」ではなく悲願の「蜂起」(Rising) にほかならなかった．だが，若き王子 Bonnie Prince Charlie を擁したジャコバイト軍は，1746年春なお浅い4月16日，Culloden Moor の凄絶な戦いにおいて，Duke of 'Butcher' Cumberland の率いるイングランド軍によって壊滅したのである．7連各8行の2行連句の詩は次の通りである．

XIII 愛国歌

The Tears of Scotland. Written in the Year 1746

Mourn, hapless Caledonia, mourn
Thy banished peace, thy laurels torn!
Thy sons, for valour long renowned,
Lie slaughtered on their native ground;
Thy hospitable roofs no more
Invite the stranger to the door;
In smoky ruins sunk they lie,
The monuments of cruelty.

嘆け,幸薄いカレドニアよ,嘆け
お前の放逐された平和を,お前の引き裂かれた月桂樹を!
お前の息子たちは,かねて武勇の誉れが高かった,
だが今は生まれ故郷の地に虐殺されて横たわる.
お前の持て成しのよい家々はもはや
見知らぬ人を戸口に招くことはない.
くすぶる廃墟のなかに崩れ横たわるのは
残虐の墓碑.

The wretched owner sees afar
His all become the prey of war;   10
Bethinks him of his babes and wife,
Then smites his breast, and curses life.
Thy swains are famished on the rocks,
Where once they fed their wanton flocks:

Thy ravished virgins shriek in vain;
Thy infants perish on the plain.

哀れな家の主(あるじ)の遙かに目に入るのは
10   彼のすべてのものが戦の餌食となるさま．
自分の赤子らや妻のことを思い，
やがて胸を打ち，人生を呪う．
お前の若者たちは岩の上で飢える，
かつては戯れる羊の群れを飼ったところだ．
お前の辱しめられた乙女たちの金切り声もむなしく，
お前の幼児らは草原に息絶える．

What boots it then, in every clime,
Through the wide-spreading waste of time,
Thy martial glory, crowned with praise,
20   Still shone with undiminished blaze?
Thy tow'ring spirit now is broke,
Thy neck is bended to the yoke.
What foreign arms could never quell,
By civil rage and rancour fell.

とすれば何の役に立とう，あらゆる国で，
時の果てしなく広がる荒廃のなか，
お前の勇ましい栄光が，賞賛に飾られて，
20   衰えを知らぬ炎で常に輝いたとしても？
お前の抜きんでた気概は今や挫かれ，

XIII 愛国歌

お前の首は軛につながれて屈した.
外国の武器ですら決して鎮圧できなかったものが,
内なる憤怒と怨恨によって倒れたのだ.

The rural pipe and merry lay
No more shall cheer the happy day:
No social scenes of gay delight
Beguile the dreary winter night:
No strains but those of sorrow flow,
And naught be heard but sounds of woe,　　　　　30
While the pale phantoms of the slain
Glide nightly o'er the silent plain.

のどかな田舎の笛や陽気な唄が
もはや幸せな日を元気づけることもない.
賑やかな喜びの社交の場景が
侘しい冬の夜を慰めることもない.
悲しみの調べのほかに歌は流れず,
苦悩の音のほかは何も聞えぬ,　　　　　30
かたや殺された者の青白い亡霊が
夜ごとに静まり返った平原をすうっと通る.

O baneful cause, oh, fatal morn,
Accursed to ages yet unborn!
The sons against their fathers stood,
The parent shed his children's blood.

Yet, when the rage of battle ceased,
The victor's soul was not appeased;
The naked and forlorn must feel
40　Devouring flames, and murd'ring steel!

おお災いを招いた大義よ,おお,致命的な朝よ,
いまだ生まれぬ後の世まで呪われてあれ!
息子たちはその父親に背き,
親はその子供らの血を流したのだ.
それだのに,戦闘の猛威が止んでも
勝者の魂は和らぐことなく,
裸で見捨てられた者たちは肌身に知るほかなかった
40　焼き尽くす焔と人殺しの鉄の剣（つるぎ）を!

The pious mother doomed to death,
Forsaken, wanders o'er the heath.
The bleak wind whistles round her head,
Her helpless orphans cry for bread;
Bereft of shelter, food, and friend,
She views the shades of night descend,
And, stretched beneath th' inclement skies,
Weeps o'er her tender babes, and dies.

信心深い母親は死の運命に定められ,
見放されて,荒野をさ迷う.
寒々とした風が頭の周りをひゅうひゅうと鳴り,

XIII 愛国歌　　　　　　　　　　213

頼るすべのない孤児たちはパンを求めて泣く.
隠れ場や, 食べ物や, 身内を奪われて,
かの母親は夜の闇が降りてくるのを眺め,
荒れ模様の空の下に長々と身を横たえて,
いとけない赤子らを想い, 泣きながら息絶える.

While the warm blood bedews my veins,
And unimpaired remembrance reigns,　　　　　　　50
Resentment of my country's fate
Within my filial breast shall beat;
And, spite of her insulting foe,
My sympathizing verse shall flow:
'Mourn, hapless Caledonia, mourn
Thy banished peace, thy laurels torn.'

　　　　　　　　　　　　　　　(1746)

熱い血がわたしの血管を濡らし,
弱まることのない追憶が支配する限り,　　　　　50
わが国の運命にたいする憤慨が
国を想う胸のうちに脈打つであろう.
そして, いかに敵が侮辱しようと,
わたしの共感の詩歌は流れるであろう.
　「嘆け, 幸薄いカレドニアよ, 嘆け
　お前の放逐された平和を, お前の引き裂かれた月桂樹を」

この後も, ジャコバイト運動の悲壮な結末に同情が続いたと

みえて，徹底した Whig ながら T. B. Macaulay 卿（1800-59）にも「あるジャコバイトの墓碑銘」（'A Jacobite Epitaph', 1845; pub. 1860)[7] と題する 18 行詩がある．マコーレーは，やはり真の正統の王のために土地も名誉も富も投げ打って献身し，再び見ることのできぬ白堊の祖国を夜ごとの夢に想いながら，異郷の大陸で男盛りに悲しみの余り髪も白く，若くして無念の死を遂げる一人のジャコバイト党員兵士を弔う追悼詩を書いたわけである．次に，この詩を挙げて「愛国歌」の結びとしよう．

A Jacobite's Epitaph

To my true king I offer'd free from stain
Courage and faith; vain faith, and courage vain.
For him I threw lands, honours, wealth, away,
And one dear hope, that was more prized than they.
For him I languish'd in a foreign clime,
Gray-hair'd with sorrow in my manhood's prime;
Heard on Lavernia Scargill's whispering trees,
And pined by Arno for my lovelier Tees;
Beheld each night my home in fever'd sleep,
Each morning started from the dream to weep;
Till God, who saw me tried too sorely, gave
The resting-place I ask'd, an early grave.
O thou, whom chance leads to this nameless stone,
From that proud country which was once mine own,

XIII 愛国歌

By those white cliffs I never more must see,
By that dear language which I spake like thee,
Forget all feuds, and shed one English tear
O'er English dust. A broken heart lies here.

注

1) *18th V*, No.193, p.290.
2) Ibid., No.194, pp.290-1.

RICHARD LEVERIDGE
1670−1758
A Song in Praise of Old English Roast Beef

WHEN mighty Roast Beef was the *Englishman*'s Food,
　　It enobled our Veins and enriched our Blood,
　Our Soldiers were brave and our Courtiers were good.
　　Oh the Roast Beef of Old England,
　　And Old English *Roast Beef.*

But since we have learn'd from all-conquering *France*
To eat their Ragouts as well as to dance,
We are fed up with nothing but vain Complaisance.
　　Oh the Roast Beef, &c.

Our Fathers of old were robust, stout, and strong,
And kept open House with good Cheer all Day long,
Which made their plump Tenants rejoice in this song,
　　Oh the Roast Beef, &c.

But now we are dwindled, to what shall I name?

A sneaking poor Race, half begotten — and tame,
Who sully those Honours that once shone in Fame.
   Oh the Roast Beef, &c.

When good Queen *Elizabeth* was on the Throne,
E'er Coffee, or Tea, and such Slip Slops were known,
The World was in Terror, if e'er she did frown.
   Oh the Roast Beef, &c.

In those Days, if Fleets did presume on the Main,
They seldom or never return'd back again,
As witness the vaunting *Armada* of *Spain.*
   Oh the Roast Beef, &c.

Oh then they had Stomachs to eat and to fight,
And when Wrongs were a-cooking to do themselves right!
But now we're a — I cou'd — but good Night.
   Oh the Roast Beef of Old England,
   And Old English Roast Beef.
                        The British Musical Miscellany, iii, 1735

3) W.A.Speck, *Literature and Society in Eighteenth Century England: Ideology, Politics, and Culture, 1680-1820* (Longman: London and New York, 1998), p.90.
4) *18th V*, No.168, pp.252-3.
   Cf. Palgrave's *Golden Treasury with Additional Poems,* Annotated Edition (Oxford University Press, 1914; rpt. 1953), pp.645-6.
5) Ibid., No.355, pp.579-80; No.356, pp.580-1.
6) *New 18th V*, No.268, pp.407-8.
7) *English V,* No.666, p.784.

また次のアンソロジーでは 'Epitaph on a Jacobite' の表題で収録されている. *The New Oxford Book of Victorian Verse*, edited by Christopher Ricks (1987; paperback 1990), No.158, p.186.

あ と が き

　若き Aldous Huxley（1894-1963）は第3詩集 *The Defeat of Youth and Other Poems*（1918）を出すなど詩人として出発し，その後も例えば卓抜な評論集 *Music at Night*（1931）のなか，その名も「夜の音楽」と題したエッセイの冒頭において，初夏の感覚的な夜景を散文詩のように描いていたが，その翌年には詩文選 *Texts and Pretexts: An Anthology with Commentaries*（Chatto and Windus, 1932; rpt.1949）を編んだ。それは科学や文明がいかに発達しようと，基本的な人間経験は不変であるとの信念に基づき，また「幸い文学の海には Palgrave, Quiller-Couch, Bridges の網から洩れた魚が沢山いる」というわけで，欧米はもちろんギリシアやローマなどの詩文まで幅広く集め，扱うテーマはハックスレー好みの神から人生百般にわたる森羅万象，百科全書的教養と鋭い批評眼のもと魅力に満ちたコメンタリーを付した異色ある詞華集であった。

　本書は，このハックスレー流アンソロジーに及ぶべくもないが，これまで伝統的に18世紀英詩の正典から洩れた詩をできるだけ多く選んだものである。とはいえ，これは単なる落穂拾いではなく，案外，隠れた歴史の証ともなっているのではなかろうか。名も無き小さな作品が必ずしも価値が低いわけではあるまい。この選集で取り上げた詩は，概して単色で素朴，理知的で散文的の譏りを免れず，高揚した感情や詩的情熱にはやや

乏しい憾みは残るとしても,いたずらに情緒に溺れ酔うことはない。ともあれ,本書は,ささやかな道案内ながら,従来の詩観に捉われず,さまざまなテーマを歌う18世紀英詩の豊饒さを示そうとした試みである。

なお翻訳については,原詩の詩行に可能な限り訳詩を対応させ,七五調のリズムを活かそうとして,口語体と文語体の併用,雅俗混淆のスタイルとなっているかもしれない。いずれにせよ,蟹が己の甲羅に似せて穴を掘るごとく,これは良くも悪くも 'An Anthology of My Own' なのである。

私事にわたるが,数年前,福岡女子大学大学院において「18世紀の英詩」と題した集中講義を行なったことがあり,本書の構想はこの機縁によるもので,このたびの小著の上梓に当たっては,開文社出版社長 安居洋一氏の度重なるご配慮とともに関係して下さった皆さんのご好意に厚くお礼を申し述べておかなければならない。

　　　　　　　　　　　　　　　平成12年(2000年) 3月
　　　　　　　　　　　　　　　　西の京,山口にて
　　　　　　　　　　　　　　　　　　　　著　者

索　　引
(Index of Authors Quoted)

Anon.,	32
Anonymous,	28, 186
Barber, Mary,	177
Burns, Robert,	96
Chudleigh, Lady Mary,	106
Collier, John,	39
Collier, Mary,	164
Cottle, Joseph,	152
Cowper, William,	207
Duck, stephen,	157
Dyer, John,	101
Fielding, Henry,	201
Gay, John,	19
Jenyns, Soame,	42
Leapor, Mary,	109
Lindsay, Lady Anne,	90
Lyttelton, George, 1st Baron,	68
Macaulay, T.B., 1st Baron,	214

More, Hannah,	138
Moss, Thomas,	181
Murry, Ann,	117
Pomfret, John,	2
Robinson, Mary,	24
Seymour, Frances, Countess of Hertford,	81
Shakespeare, William,	201
Smart, Christopher,	170
Smollett, Tobias,	208
Thomson, James,	203
Watts, Isaac,	47
Wesley, Charles,	54
West, Jane,	131
Williams, Helen Maria,	142
Winchilsea, Anne Finch, Countess of,	63

索　　　引
(Index of First Lines)

A soldier maimed and in the beggars' list	39
A youth there was possessed of every charm,	81
Brisk Chaunticleer his matins had begun,	170
But soon th'endearments of a husband cloy,	44
Cities and towns, ye haunts of wretchedness!	152
Come on, my partners in distress,	56
England, with all thy faults, I love thee still—	207
Just broke from school, pert, impudent, and raw	42
Hard is my fate, thus to want bread;	186
If Heav'n the Grateful Liberty wou'd give,	2
In Charles the Second's Golden Days	32
In such a Night, when every louder Wind	64
In vain I look around	69
Love's redeeming work is done;	54
Married, poor soul! your empire's over;	131
Mourn, hapless Caledonia, mourn	209
My dear! this morning we will take a ride,	118

Now new-vamped silks the mercer's window shows,	28
O wretch! hath madness cured thy dire despair?	178
Perish th'illiberal thought which would debase	138
Pity the sorrows of a poor old man!	181
Slaves cannot breathe in England; if their lungs	207
Soon as the harvest hath laid bare the plains,	157
This royal throne of kings, this scepter'd isle	201
To my true king I offer'd free from stain	214
'Twas on a summer noon, in Stainsford mead	101
Wee, sleeket, cowran, tim'rous beastie,	96
Welcome, dear wanderer, once more!	109
When bright Orion glitters in the skies	165
When *Britain* first, at heaven's command	204
When I survey the wond'rous Cross	52
When mighty rost Beef was the *Englishman*'s Food,	202
When Night first bids the twinkling Stars appear,	20
When the fierce Northwind with his airy Forces	48
When the sheep are in the fauld, when the cows come hame,	91
While in long exile far from you I roam,	143
Who has not waked to list the busy sounds	24
Wife and servant are the same,	106
Woman, a pleasing but a short-lived flow'r,	112

＜著者紹介＞
和田敏英　（わだ・としえ）
昭和5年　津和野に生まれる．
1957年　東京都立大学大学院人文科学研究科英文学専攻修士課程修了．
現在　山口東京理科大学教授．
〔主な著書・論文〕
「Aldous Huxleyの詩」(「英語青年」1964年2月号，Aldous Huxleyをしのぶ)
『「ガリバー旅行記」論争』(開文社出版，1983年)
『イギリス十八世紀小説論——言葉とイメージャリをめぐって』(開文社出版，1987年)
「『ガリバー旅行記』と大航海時代」(教養講演集44『人間と文化』，三愛新書144，1987年)
『スウィフトの詩』(九州大学出版会，1993年)など．

もう一つの18世紀英詩選　　(検印廃止)

2000年4月10日　初版発行

著　　者	和　田　敏　英
発　行　者	安　居　洋　一
印　刷　所	平　河　工　業　社
製　本　所	株式会社難波製本

〒160-0002　東京都新宿区坂町26

発行所　開文社出版株式会社

電話03(3358)6288番・振替00160-0-52864

ISBN4-87571-954-X C3098